FROM THE
NANCY DREW FILES

THE CASE: *A mayoral candidate is mixed up in a murder—and Nancy's looking for the smoking gun.*

CONTACT: *Working on Caroline Hill's campaign team, Nancy soon finds herself working on a case of homicide.*

SUSPECTS: *Patrick Gleason—Caroline's opponent in the race, he's the one who stands to gain the most if she takes a fall.*

Steve Hill—Caroline's bitter ex-husband, he's working hard for Gleason and would like nothing better than to see Caroline lose.

Anna Dimitros—A corrupt businesswoman prosecuted by Caroline, she vowed at the trial to exact revenge on the D.A.

Caroline Hill—Has she fooled everyone . . . including Nancy?

COMPLICATIONS: *Nancy's dedicated to Caroline Hill, and Ned's just as committed to Patrick Gleason. Can their relationship survive the River Heights campaign of crime?*

Books in The Nancy Drew Files® Series

#1   SECRETS CAN KILL
#2   DEADLY INTENT
#3   MURDER ON ICE
#4   SMILE AND SAY MURDER
#5   HIT AND RUN HOLIDAY
#6   WHITE WATER TERROR
#7   DEADLY DOUBLES
#8   TWO POINTS TO MURDER
#9   FALSE MOVES
#10 BURIED SECRETS
#11 HEART OF DANGER
#12 FATAL RANSOM
#13 WINGS OF FEAR
#14 THIS SIDE OF EVIL
#15 TRIAL BY FIRE
#16 NEVER SAY DIE
#17 STAY TUNED FOR
     DANGER
#18 CIRCLE OF EVIL
#19 SISTERS IN CRIME
#20 VERY DEADLY YOURS
#21 RECIPE FOR MURDER
#22 FATAL ATTRACTION
#23 SINISTER PARADISE
#24 TILL DEATH DO US PART
#25 RICH AND DANGEROUS
#26 PLAYING WITH FIRE
#27 MOST LIKELY TO DIE
#28 THE BLACK WIDOW
#29 PURE POISON
#30 DEATH BY DESIGN
#31 TROUBLE IN TAHITI
#32 HIGH MARKS FOR
     MALICE
#33 DANGER IN DISGUISE
#34 VANISHING ACT
#35 BAD MEDICINE
#36 OVER THE EDGE
#37 LAST DANCE
#38 THE FINAL SCENE
#39 THE SUSPECT NEXT
     DOOR
#40 SHADOW OF A DOUBT
#41 SOMETHING TO HIDE

#42 THE WRONG CHEMISTRY
#43 FALSE IMPRESSIONS
#44 SCENT OF DANGER
#45 OUT OF BOUNDS
#46 WIN, PLACE OR DIE
#47 FLIRTING WITH DANGER
#48 A DATE WITH DECEPTION
#49 PORTRAIT IN CRIME
#50 DEEP SECRETS
#51 A MODEL CRIME
#52 DANGER FOR HIRE
#53 TRAIL OF LIES
#54 COLD AS ICE
#55 DON'T LOOK TWICE
#56 MAKE NO MISTAKE
#57 INTO THIN AIR
#58 HOT PURSUIT
#59 HIGH RISK
#60 POISON PEN
#61 SWEET REVENGE
#62 EASY MARKS
#63 MIXED SIGNALS
#64 THE WRONG TRACK
#65 FINAL NOTES
#66 TALL, DARK AND
     DEADLY
#67 NOBODY'S BUSINESS
#68 CROSSCURRENTS
#69 RUNNING SCARED
#70 CUTTING EDGE
#71 HOT TRACKS
#72 SWISS SECRETS
#73 RENDEZVOUS IN ROME
#74 GREEK ODYSSEY
#75 A TALENT FOR MURDER
#76 THE PERFECT PLOT
#77 DANGER ON PARADE
#78 UPDATE ON CRIME
#79 NO LAUGHING MATTER
#80 POWER OF SUGGESTION
#81 MAKING WAVES
#82 DANGEROUS RELATIONS
#83 DIAMOND DECEIT
#84 CHOOSING SIDES

Available from ARCHWAY Paperbacks

The Nancy Drew Files™

Case 84
Choosing Sides
Carolyn Keene

AN ARCHWAY PAPERBACK
Published by POCKET BOOKS
New York   London   Toronto   Sydney   Tokyo   Singapore

AN ARCHWAY PAPERBACK *Original*

An Archway Paperback published by
POCKET BOOKS, a division of Simon & Schuster Inc.
1230 Avenue of the Americas, New York, NY 10020

Copyright © 1993 by Simon & Schuster Inc.
Produced by Mega-Books of New York, Inc.

ISBN: 0-671-73088-6

First Archway Paperback Printing June 1993

10 9 8 7 6 5 4 3 2 1

NANCY DREW, AN ARCHWAY PAPERBACK and colophon are registered trademarks of Simon & Schuster Inc.

THE NANCY DREW FILES is a trademark of Simon & Schuster Inc.

Cover art by Tricia Zimic

Printed in the U.S.A.

IL 6+

Choosing Sides

Chapter

One

GEORGE IS GOING to miss out on a great party tonight," Bess Marvin said. "Too bad she's playing in that tennis tournament in Chicago this week." She pushed back her long, blond hair, then handed a piece of masking tape to her friend Nancy Drew, who was standing on a stepladder in the front hallway of the Drews' home.

"Not to mention that she won't be around for the whole rest of the mayoral campaign," Nancy added. "George really wanted to help Caroline Hill win." She stuck the tape on the corner of the paper banner she was hanging over the arched doorway to the living room.

Caroline Hill was the district attorney of River Heights. Nancy had gotten to know her through her father, Carson Drew, a noted criminal lawyer. When Caroline decided to run for mayor,

1

Nancy and Bess had eagerly volunteered to help out.

"Well, you and I will have a great time working on Caroline's campaign, anyway. Going to the rallies"—she grinned—"meeting cute guys . . ."

"Definitely," Nancy agreed. Not that she wanted to meet anyone new. "I hope Ned can make it. He's been so busy with midterms that I haven't been able to reach him this week. I even got an answering machine so I wouldn't miss his calls, but so far he hasn't had time to phone." She blew a lock of reddish blond hair out of her eyes and gazed critically at the sign she had just hung.

Ned Nickerson, Nancy's boyfriend, was a student at Emerson College. She didn't get to see him often, and she really missed him.

Hearing footsteps on the stairs, Nancy turned to see her father coming down. He was wearing slacks and a sweater. His dark hair was graying at the temples, and he had the same blue eyes as Nancy.

"What do you think of the poster, Dad?" she asked, climbing down the ladder.

"'Caroline Hill, the Right Choice for Mayor of River Heights,'" Carson Drew read out loud. "It looks great!" He went to the closet and put on a windbreaker. "I have to run out to pick up the P.A. system for Caroline's speech tonight." Giving Nancy and Bess a warm smile, he added, "Thanks for giving up your Sunday to help get everything ready for tonight's fundraiser."

"It's been fun," Bess said. "I never knew how much went into something like this."

"It's worth the trouble. Caroline is an old friend of mine," Mr. Drew said. "We've faced each other in court a lot. I miss seeing her there since she's taken time off to campaign."

Bess sat down on the bottom step of the staircase. "It's hard to believe that in ten days, Sam Filanowski won't be mayor anymore. He's been mayor of River Heights nearly all my life."

"Fifteen years," Nancy put in. "If he hadn't had that heart attack a few months ago, I doubt he would have decided to step down."

"You're probably right," Mr. Drew said. He glanced at his watch. "It's nearly five. I have to run."

A few minutes later, Hannah Gruen, the Drews' housekeeper, poked her head around the kitchen door. The cheerful, gray-haired woman had lived with the Drews since Nancy was three, and she was just like family to Nancy and her father.

"Nancy, someone just pulled up in the driveway," Hannah said. She nodded toward the poster over the living-room doorway. "Oh, that looks nice!"

"Thanks," Nancy said, grinning. "Come on, Bess. I bet that's Hector. He said he was going to stop by with all the freebies for tonight."

As the two girls hurried out the front door, Nancy saw Hector Alvarez, Caroline's campaign manager, pulling two cardboard boxes out of the trunk of his car. He had black curly hair and a compact build.

"What's in the boxes?" Bess asked, taking one of them from him and heading back to the house. Hector and Nancy followed, with Hector carrying the second box.

"Open them up, open them up!" Hector bubbled. He set his box down next to Bess's in the foyer. "I want to hear what you two experts think of the stuff we'll be giving away at the fundraiser tonight."

Nancy was already tearing open one box. She pulled out a neon green T-shirt and held it up. Huge block letters across the front read: THE ANSWER: HILL FOR MAYOR.

"Intense!" she exclaimed.

"Everyone's going to love those," Bess agreed.

Hector grinned. Then he opened the other box and started digging through it. "I've got Hill for Mayor caps in lots of colors, too. Here, try this."

He handed Bess a neon orange cap. She put the hat on and turned to look at her reflection in the small mirror next to the Drews' front door. "Cool!"

Turning to Hector, Nancy asked, "How do the polls look? Have you gotten the latest results?"

"Sure did," he replied, his dark eyes crinkling in a smile. "We're beating Patrick Gleason by ten points."

"Great!" Nancy and Bess said together.

"But we're not in the clear," Hector cautioned. "I happen to know that Gleason is doing a media blitz this week. He's spent a lot of money on TV and radio commercials. Election day is a week from Tuesday. We've got to keep hustling."

"That means tonight's fundraiser is really important," Nancy said. "If Caroline wants to compete with Gleason's ads, she'll need to raise a lot of money. I've just been assuming that Caroline would win."

"You know," Bess said, "my dad works with Patrick Gleason on the city council. Dad says that Gleason is a good guy but that Caroline would make a better mayor."

"Everyone likes Gleason," Nancy pointed out. "He's got three kids, and he's a former basketball star and coach at Emerson College. . . ." Her voice trailed off.

Hector looked from Nancy to Bess. "You two are acting as if the election is over and lost. Cheer up! Tonight's party is going to be great, and next week we'll be celebrating!"

"Bess, why don't you take a break," Nancy said a few hours later. "I'll take over for a while." She and Bess had been passing out trays of hors d'oeuvres since guests had started arriving an hour earlier.

"Okay, if you're sure. I wouldn't mind taking a break to listen to Caroline's speech."

Just then Carson Drew's amplified voice rose over the din in the crowded living room. "Ladies and gentlemen, could I have your attention, please!"

As Bess went to return her empty tray to the kitchen, Nancy stood on tiptoe to spot her father through the crowd. He was standing at the far end of the room.

When the crowd quieted down, Mr. Drew said, "Although we were often opponents in the courtroom, I have always had nothing but the highest regard for Caroline Hill's integrity, moral strength, and sharp mind. These qualities, combined with her knowledge of city government and environmental law, make her the only logical choice for the mayor of River Heights. But Caroline is here to speak for herself. Ladies and gentlemen, Caroline Hill!"

The crowd clapped loudly and cleared a space as an attractive woman in her early forties stepped forward. She had sleek, chin-length brown hair and large hazel eyes, and she was wearing a plum-colored linen coatdress. Nancy had to admire her cool, professional style.

"I am here tonight because I believe in the future of River Heights," Caroline began in a clear, sure voice. She went on to list her plans for bringing recycling to the town, increasing public transportation, and cleaning up the Muskoka River. Everyone was silent as she spoke, but the whole house erupted in cheers and applause when she finished.

Nancy grinned as everyone crowded around Caroline and started talking enthusiastically. Several people were taking out their checkbooks. It looked as if the fundraiser was going to be a success!

As Nancy started to work her way through the crowd with her tray of fried wontons, a familiar voice spoke up behind her.

"Excuse me, miss. I'm looking for a gorgeous young redhead, about your height?"

Nancy spun around. "Ned, you're here!" she cried, looking at her handsome boyfriend. He was wearing a white shirt and khaki pants, and his wavy brown hair was still damp from a recent shower. Nancy stood on her toes to kiss him.

"I don't know if the staff should be kissing the guests," he joked when they pulled apart, "but I kind of like it."

"How are you, Ned?" Nancy said in a rush. "How did all your midterms go? You look a little tired." She reached up with her free hand and lightly touched the dark circles under his eyes.

Ned chuckled and helped himself to a fried wonton from her tray. "I'm beat," he admitted, "but everything went fine. I think I even aced a couple of tests." He looked around the room.

"But you didn't have to throw a party just for me, Drew."

"Anything for you, Nickerson," Nancy replied, grinning.

"No, really," Ned said. "Who's this party for?"

Nancy frowned. "Didn't your roommate tell you? I left a message——" she began.

"Ease up," he said lightly, reaching for another wonton. "We haven't had time to do anything but study and write papers. You should see my pile of dirty laundry!"

Nancy relaxed. "Sorry, Ned," she said. "It's just that I've been so wrapped up in this election."

"I know what you mean. Something tells me that I'm not going to be getting a lot of rest until election day."

Nancy was puzzled. "So you do know about the election?"

"Sure."

"Then your roommate *did* tell you," Nancy insisted.

Now Ned looked confused. "Tell me what?"

"That I'm working for Caroline Hill," Nancy said impatiently. "This party is a fundraiser for her campaign."

Ned's pleasant expression faded. "Are you telling me that you're working *against* Patrick Gleason?"

8

Nancy laughed nervously. "Of course. I want Caroline Hill to be elected. Don't you?"

"Not at all," Ned said coolly. "As a matter of fact, I've already told Patrick Gleason that I'm going to help out with *his* campaign!"

Nancy stared open-mouthed at Ned. She couldn't believe what she was hearing. Her boyfriend was working for the opposition!

Chapter

Two

For a moment, all Nancy could do was stare at Ned. Finally, he cleared his throat and spoke.

"Nancy, I know Patrick Gleason. He used to play basketball at Emerson, and he was a coach. There are a whole crew of Emerson students who are helping out on his campaign, even though a lot of us don't live in River Heights. Everyone's got a lot of admiration for him. He's come around to help our team out, and I've had some good conversations with him. I realize that you must feel the same way about Caroline Hill, and I can respect that." He squeezed her shoulder gently.

Ned's fairness was one of the things that Nancy loved about him. She smiled, feeling a little better. "You're right about respecting each other, that's the most important thing," she said. "We

10

can't always agree on everything." Leaning closer to him, she said softly, "Do you realize you're in the enemy's camp? I could turn you in for spying, you know."

Ned laughed and looked around the room. "Actually, maybe I *shouldn't* be here," he told her. "I wouldn't want to embarrass you."

"You could never embarrass me, Nickerson," she said, standing on tiptoe to kiss his cheek. "But I do have to get busy. Bess is around here somewhere. I'll find you guys in a little while, okay?"

It took only a few minutes to pass out the remaining wontons on her tray. She was about to head back to the kitchen when Caroline broke away from a small group to greet her. "This is the first chance I've had all night to thank you," Caroline said.

Nancy smiled. "I'm happy to help out. I thought your speech was—"

"Excuse me," an older man interrupted. He was in his late sixties, Nancy guessed, with a short but powerful build, widely spaced pale gray eyes, graying blond hair, and a no-nonsense expression. The man looked past Nancy at Caroline.

"Mr. Blount, I'm so glad you could come tonight," Caroline said, smiling politely.

"Thank you," he said in a deep, gravelly voice. "I must say, I'm very impressed by your campaign so far. I can see that you care as much about River Heights as I do. I'm afraid I have to leave now, but first I'd like to make a small contribution to your cause." He shook her hand and pressed a check into it, then said goodbye and walked away.

Caroline studied the check. "Wow, that's a lot of ice cream!" she exclaimed, her eyes widening.

Glancing at the check, Nancy saw that it was for five thousand dollars. "Talk about generous!" Nancy agreed. "But what does ice cream have to do with anything?"

Caroline folded the check and slipped it into her dress pocket. "That was Alan Blount. He made a fortune with his ice cream company in Chicago before he retired to River Heights about ten years ago. He really does love this town. He's the one who donated a new wing to the hospital last year. I'm sure glad he's on our side."

Before Caroline could say anything more, Hector appeared and whisked her off to talk to more supporters. Nancy passed out a few more trays of food, then decided to take a break. She found Ned and Bess standing next to the fireplace in the living room.

"Bess, you mean to say that in this house packed with people, you don't see a single guy you're interested in?" Ned was asking, a teasing glint in his brown eyes.

Bess looked at her friends and sighed. "Sad but true. There's not a cute guy in the whole room who's under thirty."

12

"I guess most kids our age don't have money to throw around at fundraisers. . . ." Nancy said. Her voice trailed off as she spotted a newcomer who'd just entered the house. "Or maybe I spoke too soon. Hold on, I'll be right back."

Nancy quickly made her way to the foyer, where a tall guy in his early twenties was standing. He had short, curly blond hair, high cheekbones, and a cleft chin. He was with a girl who had brown eyes and curly auburn hair.

"Kyle, I'm glad you came!" Nancy said, taking their jackets and squeezing them into the hall closet. She had met Kyle Donovan at her father's law firm, where he had just started as a paralegal. Besides being cute, she knew that Kyle was also really nice—just the kind of guy Bess would go crazy over. But who was the girl with him?

"Are you kidding? I wouldn't miss this," Kyle told Nancy, smiling. He put a friendly arm around the auburn-haired girl and added, "Nancy, this is my sister, Mary."

"Your sister? Great! I mean, nice to meet you," Nancy said, shaking hands with her. "Why don't you two come with me? I want to introduce you to my friends."

Mary hesitated. "I hate to be rude, but I promised my boyfriend I'd call as soon as we got here. Is there a phone I could use?"

"No problem. There's a phone in the kitchen, through that door." After Mary disappeared into the kitchen, Nancy led Kyle over to Ned and

13

Bess. When she introduced them, Nancy didn't miss the quick glimmer of interest in Bess's blue eyes. Then, just as quickly, the glimmer disappeared.

Nancy wasn't sure why Bess was acting so cool.

"Kyle, are you in college?" Ned asked.

"Uh, no, just graduated," Kyle replied, pulling his gaze away from Bess. "I'm working as a paralegal for Mr. Drew—I'm saving up for law school. But I'm taking some time off this week to work on the Hill campaign. We figured that with the election down to the wire, Caroline needs all the help she can get."

Nancy glanced quizzically at Bess. She had thought that her friend would be attracted to Kyle. He was handsome, smart, and interesting. But Bess was just staring off into space. Kyle, on the other hand, couldn't take his eyes off Bess, even while he and Ned discussed his plans for law school. Suddenly, Bess excused herself. As she headed out of the room, Kyle followed her with his eyes.

"Did I say something wrong?" Kyle asked, turning back to Nancy.

Nancy shrugged. "Let me see if I can find out what's bothering her."

She caught up to Bess in the hallway. "Bess, why were you so cold to Kyle?"

"He has a lot of nerve!" Bess burst out. "Did you see the way he looked at me?"

"Hold it," Nancy said. "Since when is it a crime for a guy to smile at you?"

Bess looked insulted. "I can't believe you're saying this. I mean, sure, he's cute and all, but I saw him at the door with his girlfriend! If you ask me, it's pretty rude of him to flirt with me the second she's not around."

Nancy burst into laughter.

"I don't see what's so funny about that!"

"I'm sorry, Bess. I should have realized," Nancy began. "The person you thought was his girlfriend is actually his *sister.*"

A look of horror crossed Bess's face. "His sister?" she gasped. "I am such a jerk! Nancy, he must think I'm awful!"

"I'm sure you could convince him otherwise," Nancy replied, raising an eyebrow. "He definitely seems interested in you."

"Do you think so?" Bess paused, then grinned. "He really is gorgeous, isn't he?"

"Well, I'm relieved to see the old Bess back," Nancy joked. "You had me worried there."

"Well, what are we waiting for? Let's go back so I can talk to him!"

The next morning Nancy arrived at Caroline Hill's headquarters at nine o'clock. For the past week, she and Bess had answered phones, run errands, and generally done whatever was needed. As she glanced around the crowded storefront headquarters, Nancy saw that Bess hadn't arrived yet. About a dozen other volunteers were scattered about, talking on the phones and stuffing publicity pamphlets into envelopes. Nancy was just going over to help with the pamphlets when Bess walked in, singing softly to herself.

"It looked like you and Kyle hit it off last night," Nancy said, grinning at her friend.

"Did we ever!" Bess sighed happily. "He asked me out for Tuesday night! Luckily, he's working in your dad's office this morning. If he was here, I wouldn't be able to concentrate on anything else but him."

"Looks like you've got it bad, Bess," Nancy commented. "But before we lose you altogether, let's ask Caroline if she wants us to do anything for tonight's rally." A big rally for Caroline was being held at the high school that evening, and Nancy had a feeling there would be last-minute details to take care of.

Nancy led the way to a doorway at the rear of the room that led to Caroline's tiny office. Hector was already there, standing in front of Caroline's desk and talking on her phone. Caroline was sitting behind the desk, looking at some papers.

"Great party last night, Nancy," Hector said with a smile as he hung up the phone. "Hi, Bess."

"You two were a tremendous help," Caroline added, glancing up from her desk. "Thanks again."

"No problem," Nancy replied. "I thought it—"

She broke off as a woman pushed through the doorway, almost knocking down Nancy and Bess.

"Whoa!" Bess exclaimed, stumbling.

"Have you seen this yet?" the woman asked urgently, shoving a newspaper at Hector.

Hector took one glance at the paper, and his face turned white. "Oh, no!" he exclaimed.

Nancy exchanged a worried look with Bess.

"Hector, what is it?" Caroline asked, a note of tenseness creeping into her voice.

Hector handed the newspaper to Caroline. As the candidate spread it out on her desk, Nancy twisted her head around to look at the headline: "Caroline Caught with Cold Cash. Mayoral Hopeful Finances Fencing Ring!"

A shiver of shock ran through Nancy as she looked at the grainy photograph below the headline. The photo showed a woman handing money to a seedy-looking guy. There was no mistaking the woman's face—it was Caroline Hill!

Chapter

Three

CAROLINE!" Nancy exclaimed. "They're calling you a criminal!"

"This is awful!" Bess cried.

"Of all the outrageous stunts," Caroline spat out. She looked around the room, meeting everyone's gaze directly. "I want you all to know that this story is completely false. Someone is trying to frame me!"

"What exactly does the story say?" Bess asked.

Caroline looked back at the paper and read the article out loud. " 'Caroline Hill began her association with Bobby Rouse, seen in the photograph with Hill, when Hill prosecuted him two years ago for armed robbery.' "

She looked up and frowned. "I remember that case. Unfortunately, we didn't have enough evidence to convict Rouse." Turning back to the paper, she read on. "'Later, according to a reputable source, Rouse and Hill became partners in a fencing ring for stolen electronics.'"

Hector had been reading ahead. "The article says you gave Rouse money to buy electronics that had been stolen from warehouses," he explained. "Then he sold them for a higher price, and you two split the money."

"It's all lies!" Caroline said angrily.

Nancy noticed that a crowd of volunteers and staff members had gathered outside the office doorway. Everyone was talking and asking questions.

"Someone's out to frame you, Caroline," a young guy said.

There were loud cries of agreement, but one woman said, "What about the photograph? It sure looks real."

"All right, everyone. Calm down and let's get back to work," Hector said, waving everyone away from the doorway. "This story is false, of course. I'm going to get on the phone to the paper right away to issue a denial."

Nancy glanced at the article again, and for the first time she noticed the byline. "Bess, look. Brenda Carlton reported this story!"

"That figures." Bess rolled her eyes.

"You know her?" Caroline asked.

Nancy nodded. "Brenda's father owns *Today's*

19

Times. He lets her report for the paper, but she's not exactly the most experienced professional on their staff."

"Hey, Nan, maybe we could talk to Brenda instead of Hector," Bess suggested. "Since we know her, we might have a better chance of finding out what really happened."

"Sounds good," Hector agreed.

Nancy saw that Caroline was still glaring at the newspaper article. "This woman is wearing a flowered dress. I never wear flowered prints!"

Nancy looked at the photo again. "Something's not right about this," she said slowly slowly. She looked at Caroline, noticing for the first time the silver bracelet that the candidate wore. "How long have you worn that medical bracelet?"

Caroline glanced at her wrist. "Since I was eighteen. Why?"

"And you never take it off?" Nancy asked.

"Of course not, I'm diabetic."

Nancy felt a wave of relief. "The woman in the photograph isn't wearing one. That *proves* that this picture is a fake!"

Hector, Bess, and Caroline all leaned over the paper. Sure enough, the woman had no bracelet on the wrist of her bare, outstretched arm.

"Nancy, you're a genius!" Caroline exclaimed.

"Great. Now we have proof. I'd better work on a statement to give the media right away." Hector took a pad from Caroline's desk and began writing.

"Nancy, my staff is going to be working overtime countering this accusation," Caroline said. "I know you volunteered to help campaign, but I could really use a good detective to get to the bottom of this, and your dad tells me you're the best. Do you think you could find time to look into the story?"

"Sure thing," Nancy replied.

"I could help, too," Bess offered. "If you want me to, that is."

Caroline flashed a smile at Bess. "Great idea."

"We'd better go over everything you know first," Nancy said. She and Bess pulled two wooden chairs up to Caroline's desk and sat down. "Can you think of anyone who would want to ruin your campaign?" Nancy asked.

Caroline frowned and shook her head.

"I can think of someone," Hector put in quietly. "Patrick Gleason."

"That's a serious charge, Hector, one that I'm not willing to make yet," Caroline said.

Neither am I, Nancy thought. Especially with Ned working on his campaign. She looked at Hector. "Do you have any reason to suspect Gleason, other than the fact that he's the opponent?"

"An opponent who has a losing campaign," Hector said forcefully.

21

Just then the phone rang, and Hector picked it up. "It's Channel Nine, WRVH," he whispered to Caroline, covering the mouthpiece. "They want to interview you about the article. I'll talk to them in the other room."

Caroline nodded grimly. She rubbed her temples as her campaign manager left the office. Obviously, the article had upset her.

"Tell me about Bobby Rouse," Nancy said.

Caroline leaned back in her chair. "He's been arrested several times for stealing cars and robbing stores. From what I remember, he usually works for other people, not on his own."

"So maybe someone else put him up to posing for this picture," Nancy said. "But who?"

"I haven't thought about Bobby Rouse since the trial two years ago," she said wearily. "I'll dig up his files and see if I find any names."

Bess leaned forward in her chair and asked, "Maybe Nancy and I could try talking to him to see what we can find out, too. Do you have any idea where we could find him?"

"We might have an address in his files, but that information is two years old. Maybe you should try the police," Caroline replied. "Rouse has a long record, so they might have more recent information."

"I'll give Chief McGinnis a call," Nancy said. "But first, Bess and I are going to visit Brenda to get her to print a retraction. Hopefully, we'll be able to get some info about her source, too. If I know her, she'll be dying to talk about her big scoop."

Ten minutes later Bess and Nancy were on their way to the *Today's Times* office in Nancy's blue Mustang. Bess was staring at a copy of the article that Nancy had taken from Caroline's campaign headquarters. "I mean, I know it's a fake, but how did the person who made it get it to look so convincing?"

"Bobby Rouse must have posed for a picture where he was accepting money from *another* woman," Nancy said. "Then someone took an old photo of Caroline and cut out just her head, pasting it over the other woman's body in the photo. That way, it would look as if *Caroline* were the person handing the money to Rouse."

"But wouldn't that look obviously fake?" Bess asked, giving Nancy a dubious glance.

Nancy nodded as she turned her Mustang left onto the main drag of downtown River Heights. "Yes. But if someone took a new photograph of the pieced-together picture, they could easily touch up the negative to make it look natural. That way the person could make another, almost perfect-looking print with the new negative."

"Wow." Bess shook her head in amazement. "It sounds as if someone went to a lot of trouble to frame Caroline."

"That's for sure. I just hope we can find out who."

"But how can you be sure Rouse actually *posed* for the photo?" Bess asked. "I mean, he has a record. Isn't it possible someone got hold of an old photograph of him accepting a bribe, then put Caroline's head on the woman's body? Maybe Rouse himself had nothing to do with this picture."

"I thought about that, too," Nancy said. "But it looks set up. It's been taken right out in the open, and the woman has her arm stretched out so that no one could miss the fact that she's giving him a wad of bills. I'm positive the photo was staged."

Nancy pulled into the *Today's Times* parking lot and found a spot. Then she and Bess headed into the brick building and took the elevator up to the newsroom. Reporters sat at their desks, clicking away on their computers and talking on phones. Brenda was at her desk near the far end of the room.

"Check it out, Nan," Bess said in a low voice. "It looks as if Brenda has adopted the Serious Journalist look."

Brenda's long, dark hair was pulled back in a neat bun, Nancy saw. She wore a tailored wool suit with a crisp white blouse instead of her usual, more feminine clothes. Brenda was talking on the phone, but when she saw Nancy and Bess, she motioned for them to sit down in the two chairs by her desk.

"This scoop is already opening doors for me," Brenda said into the phone. "You won't believe who I'm interviewing on Friday: Mayor Filanowski! I'm the only one who's managed to get an interview with him. He was genuinely impressed by my story." Brenda paused. "Well, he *did* set conditions. He still won't discuss the election or the candidates, but I'm sure I can get him to."

"That's Brenda," Bess whispered in Nancy's ear. "Humble as always."

Brenda hung up the phone and gave her visitors a smug smile. "I'm glad you stopped by," she said. "Being congratulated by Nancy Drew, ace detective, means a lot to me."

"Actually, Brenda," Nancy said, ignoring the reporter's arch tone, "Bess and I are here to ask you to print a retraction to your story. I'm sure you didn't—"

"A what!" Brenda shrieked.

Glancing at Brenda's desk, Nancy saw a copy of the article about Caroline Hill. "That photo is a fake," she said, pointing to it. "Caroline Hill has worn a medical ID bracelet constantly for years, but the woman in this photo doesn't have one. That woman isn't Caroline Hill at all—the photo's just been doctored to make it look as if she is."

"You're making that up." Brenda sniffed. "You're jealous because for once *I* beat *you* to uncovering a big crime. Besides, I have the original photograph right here to prove you're wrong."

Brenda shuffled through the papers on her desk and handed Nancy a manila envelope. Nancy slid out an eight-by-ten black and white photograph.

"Brenda, this doesn't prove anything," she argued. "Did you meet the person who gave you this photo and told you about the fencing ring?"

"What do you think? Of course I met him!" Brenda replied indignantly. She glanced warily at Nancy and Bess. "Don't even bother trying to find out who it is. You should both know that as a journalist I'm protected by the First Amendment. I'll never reveal my sources."

Nancy tried not to let her frustration show. "But, Brenda, the story is a lie. The person who gave you this information was breaking the law."

"Which means you're protecting a criminal, not the truth," Bess added forcefully.

Brenda still didn't look convinced. "How do you two know that Caroline Hill wore that bracelet constantly?" she shot back. "For all you know, *she's* lying!"

Nancy could see that Brenda wasn't going to be helpful. She was just about to slide the photograph back into its envelope when she noticed something on the reverse side. It looked as if something had been written down, then erased.

Squinting at the slight indentations, Nancy

tried to make out the words. The first word was "Contact." And beneath it two telephone numbers were listed. Nancy quickly memorized the numbers, then replaced the photograph in the envelope and handed it back to Brenda.

"Well, I guess I misjudged you," Nancy said, getting up. She wanted to leave before she forgot those numbers! "Come on, Bess, let's go."

Bess looked startled, but she stood and followed Nancy from the newsroom. "Why did you let her get away with that?" she whispered as soon as they were out of Brenda's earshot.

Nancy was muttering the numbers to herself. Just outside the newsroom, she stopped abruptly to write them down in the small notebook she carried in her shoulder bag. "I didn't, Bess, not exactly. I still think we should tell Mr. Carlton about the doctored photo. Even if you and I can't get Brenda to print a retraction, her own father can."

She pointed to the numbers she'd just written down. "But first, I have to call these phone numbers. Brenda wrote them on the back of the photo, and I'm pretty sure they're the numbers for the person who gave her the photo and the story."

In the lobby they found a pay phone. After digging in her bag for change, Nancy dialed the first number. There was no answer.

"Try the other number," Bess encouraged. She bit her lip expectantly as Nancy fished her quarter from the change slot, fed it in again, and dialed.

The phone rang several times. Nancy was about to hang up, when someone answered.

"Hello," a cheerful man's voice answered. "Patrick Gleason's campaign headquarters. How may I help you?"

Chapter

Four

NANCY OPENED HER MOUTH, but no words came out. She slammed the phone down, stunned.

"Nancy, what is it?" Bess asked.

"That second number is for Patrick Gleason's headquarters!" Nancy said.

Bess's eyes widened. "Do you think *Gleason* is the one who's trying to frame Caroline?" she asked. "Patrick Gleason may not be the best choice for mayor, but I never heard my dad say anything about him being sleazy enough to do something like *this.*"

"From what Ned says, he's a really honest guy," Nancy agreed. "But if he's desperate enough to win the election . . ." Her voice trailed off. Then she said, "Or maybe someone who's working on Gleason's campaign gave Brenda the scoop. It's possible that Gleason doesn't know anything about it. Anyway," she continued, "at least we have a lead. Ned said he was going to be working on Gleason's campaign today. After we talk to Brenda's father, I'm going to go over to Gleason's headquarters and see what I can find out."

"What should I do?" Bess asked.

Nancy thought for a moment. "Maybe you should go back to Caroline's office and tell her and Hector about this lead. I'll drop you off and meet you back there when I'm finished."

"Sure," Bess agreed. Her blue eyes sparkled as she added, "Besides, Kyle said he was going to be around this afternoon."

Half an hour later, Nancy pulled her Mustang to a halt in front of the downtown storefront where Patrick Gleason had his campaign office. She got out of her car and peered through the huge plate-glass windows plastered with Gleason posters.

The place seemed just as chaotic as Caroline's headquarters. Nancy didn't spot Ned, but it looked as if half of Emerson College had volunteered to help.

Nancy felt a little nervous as she stepped inside. What if someone recognized her as a volunteer for Caroline Hill's campaign?

"Hi!" Two lanky guys about Nancy's age greeted her immediately. Their button-down shirts were covered with "Gleason for Mayor" buttons. "Are you here to volunteer for the campaign?" one guy asked.

"Uh, no," Nancy replied. "I'm here to see Ned Nickerson."

"He's over there, answering phones." The other guy pointed across the room to a corner that hadn't been visible from the window. Ned had a telephone receiver to his ear. He looked so preoccupied that Nancy hesitated to interrupt him.

She was crossing toward him, when a door opened at the rear of the office and a man wearing a suit walked out. He was over six feet tall, lean and handsome, with a short, thick shock of dark hair that gave him a boyish air. Nancy recognized Patrick Gleason from his posters. He headed toward the water fountain near Nancy and stooped to get a drink.

Taking a deep breath, Nancy strode over to the candidate. "Hello, Mr. Gleason," she began in a cheerful, brisk voice, "I'm Nancy Drew, Ned Nickerson's girlfriend."

Patrick Gleason spun around, and a dazzling smile flashed across his face. "It's a pleasure to meet you, Nancy," he said, shaking her hand firmly. "Ned's talked a lot about you. He mentioned that you're working for Caroline Hill," Gleason added with a note of amusement. "That must make for interesting dinner conversation."

"It does." Nancy took a deep breath before adding, "Particularly with the ridiculous allegation against Caroline Hill that was in *Today's Times* this morning. You wouldn't happen to know who gave that story to the paper, would you?"

Gleason's smile faded. He took Nancy's arm and ushered her into his office. "Are you accusing me of planting stories about my opponent?" he demanded, shutting the door.

Nancy swept her eyes over the clutter on Gleason's desk. She didn't see anything to indicate that he had provided Brenda with the story. "I have reason to believe that someone from this—"

Her words were cut short when Gleason's intercom was buzzed, and a voice said, "Brodsky from the *Morning Record* is on line three."

"Sorry," Patrick Gleason told Nancy, but his expression was more relieved than apologetic. He opened the door again and gestured the way out. "We'll talk again, I'm sure."

"Just let me—" Nancy began, but Gleason was already on the phone.

Sighing, she stepped out of his office. As she was heading over to Ned, a voice behind Nancy caught her ear. "Hill should drop out now. She'll never live this down!"

Glancing over her shoulder, Nancy saw that a big, beefy guy was talking to two other young men. She was angry, but she didn't say anything. She didn't want to draw attention to the fact that she was a Caroline Hill supporter.

Nancy was a few feet from Ned when he hung up his phone and noticed her. "Nancy!" He grinned, stood up, and kissed her over the desk. "What are you doing here?"

"Hi, Ned," Nancy replied. He looked so cute that she felt her irritation fade immediately. "Can we talk somewhere?"

Ned nodded and led her to an empty table. "I saw that story about Caroline's fencing ring in the paper," he said quietly. "It isn't true, is it?"

"No, it's not," Nancy replied. "I'm glad you haven't assumed that it is, the way other people around here apparently have." She glanced over her shoulder at the three men she had overheard.

"Oh, those guys." Ned dismissed the group with a wave of his hand. "They have a bad attitude. They're working for Gleason just because they don't want a woman to be mayor."

"They sound like total jerks," Nancy muttered. Turning her mind back to the case, she told Ned about the events of the morning, including the phone numbers she'd spotted on the back of Brenda's copy of the picture.

"When I dialed the second number, someone from *this* office answered the phone," Nancy finished.

"From here? But who would that be?"

"What about Gleason? Do you think he could be involved at all?" Nancy asked.

Ned's eyebrows shot up. "Gleason? No way!" he said emphatically. "I mean, I guess it makes

33

sense to suspect him, but he just wouldn't do something like that, I'm sure of it."

"It could be someone who works here," Nancy said. She wanted to believe her boyfriend, but she couldn't be sure he was right until she found out who *was* responsible. "Just promise me you'll keep your eyes and ears open, okay?"

After a slight hesitation, Ned said, "I can't say I like the idea of spying on my boss, but if that's the only way to prove he's innocent . . ."

"Thanks, Ned," Nancy said, standing up. "I've got to run now."

As Ned was walking her to the door, a thin man in his forties, with wispy red hair and wire-rimmed glasses, came in. Once he had walked past Nancy and Ned, Ned leaned close to Nancy. "Do you recognize that guy?" he whispered.

Nancy took a second look at the man, then shook her head.

"That's Steve Hill, Caroline Hill's ex-husband. Today is his first day as a volunteer. He's actually using his vacation time to work here." Ned chuckled. "I heard that he's working for Gleason because he doesn't want his ex-wife to be his new boss. He's a tax accountant for the city."

"No kidding!" Nancy looked at Steve Hill with fresh interest. "If he doesn't like her that much, maybe *he's* the one who gave the photo to Brenda."

"But why would he implicate Gleason by giving Brenda this number?" Ned pointed out.

"I don't know." Nancy sighed. "It's just an idea. But if you wouldn't mind . . ."

"I know, I know," Ned said, holding up a hand. "I'll keep an eye on him. Now get out of here before you have me tapping all the phones!"

"When I got a job with your father, I didn't realize I'd end up hot on the trail of criminals with you, Nancy," Kyle Donovan said from the backseat of Nancy's car an hour later.

Bess turned to grin at him from the front seat. "It's a required part of being friends with Nancy," she said. "Don't worry, you'll get used to it."

Bess and Kyle had been folding leaflets when Nancy returned to Caroline's campaign office. After filling in her friends and Caroline on all that had happened, the three decided to track down Bobby Rouse.

Caroline had checked out her files on Rouse. There was no current address, but the files mentioned a diner where Bobby Rouse had been known to spend a lot of time. Nancy had called Chief McGinnis, and he had confirmed that it was one of Rouse's regular hangouts. If he came up with any more information on him, the police chief promised to call Nancy with it at Caroline's headquarters.

"Here we are," Nancy announced, pulling up

across the street from a small, dingy diner on the outskirts of River Heights. "Slim and Shorty's Good Eats Café," Nancy said, reading the sign over the door.

She did a double-take as two men stepped out of the café. One was tall and lanky. Nancy recognized the other, shorter man immediately from Caroline's files on Bobby Rouse.

"Hey, that's him!" she said to Bess and Kyle. "The shorter guy. You two wait here while I try to talk to Rouse, okay?"

"Okay," Bess said, "but be careful."

Nancy was already halfway out of the car. As she crossed the street, she heard Rouse say, "See ya, Ralph" to the taller guy. Then he got into a sleek new black sports car, while his friend got into a brown sedan.

Nancy hurried over to the sports car. "Hi," she said in her best, harmless teenager voice, resting a hand on his open window. "I was wondering if I could ask you a question?"

Rouse looked up at her in alarm. "I've had it with you people!" he growled. "I'm warning you, stay away from me!" With that, he turned on the ignition and revved the motor.

"I know about the doctored photograph of Caroline Hill, and I think you were set up, Bobby!" Nancy yelled over the noise, saying anything that might make him want to talk to her. "I want to find out who did it. And why!"

Bobby Rouse ignored her. He threw the sports

car into gear, and Nancy stumbled backward as he peeled away, leaving the stench of burning rubber in his wake.

"Rats!" Nancy kicked at the pavement, then ran back to her Mustang and jumped behind the wheel.

"He wouldn't listen," Nancy said as she started the car. She made a U-turn, then headed after the black car. "We've got to move fast, or we'll lose him."

Rouse was driving back toward town. Nancy followed as quickly as she dared.

"Hold on, guys!" she called to Bess and Kyle as she followed the black sports car around a sharp right turn. The Mustang toppled a garbage can as they spun around into an alley. Up ahead, Rouse's car was fishtailing out of the alley. Nancy's heart pounded as she raced after him, rounded a corner, and headed down a deserted brick paved street. She floored the gas pedal.

Just as Nancy was beginning to wonder where Rouse was leading her, he turned into a construction site.

"Where is he taking us?" Kyle asked through clenched teeth as the Mustang whipped past huge piles of sand, cinder blocks, and metal beams. An idle bulldozer and a crane sat off to one side of a gaping hole that seemed to take up an entire block. It was ringed with a flimsy wooden fence.

Just then Rouse's sports car nicked one edge of a stack of bricks that were covered with a black plastic tarp. The impact sent the tarp flying into the air. It landed on the Mustang's windshield!

"I can't see a thing!" Nancy cried. Panicked, she took her foot off the gas and pumped the brakes. She frantically lowered her window, reached out, and pulled the tarp off.

"Nancy, look out!" Bess screamed.

Nancy gasped. They were headed straight for the cavernous construction hole!

She slammed harder on her brakes. Her tires dug into the powdery dirt, but it was too late. The Mustang crashed through the fence and spun around in a half circle. Terrified, she felt the back of her car slip over the edge of the hole.

In a second, the car was going to plunge into the abyss!

Chapter

Five

NANCY FELT her stomach lurch as the Mustang teetered dangerously at the edge of the construction pit. She hardly dared to breathe. The right rear tire had already slipped over the edge. Even though the car had stopped, she knew it could still slip backward.

"Nancy, that hole must be forty feet deep!" Bess said in a horrified whisper. "What are we going to do?" She gasped as the ground beneath the rear left wheel crumbled and the car shuddered and tipped downward a little more. "Oh, no! We're falling in!"

"Hold still, Bess, you're rocking the car!" Kyle said from the backseat. Looking at him in the rearview mirror, Nancy saw that his face was tight with fear.

Nancy took a deep breath. "I'm going to try to

39

pull us up and out of here by moving forward very gently. Don't move at all, or we might slide backward."

Next to Nancy, Bess closed her eyes tightly. "Tell me when it's over," she whispered.

Trying not to think about how deep the pit was, Nancy took her foot off the brake and pressed it ever so lightly on the gas pedal. Her heart jumped as the left rear wheel slipped again. Then to her amazement, the Mustang pulled slowly forward, away from the pit.

A moment later Nancy felt the rear tires take hold on solid ground. She exhaled the breath she'd been holding and felt a cold sweat break out on her forehead. With the car a safe distance from the pit, she killed the engine and slumped back against the seat.

"Nancy, you did it!" Kyle said in a shaky voice. "Boy, for a minute there, I really thought we were history."

"Can we just get out of here?" Bess asked, opening her eyes.

Nancy looked in the direction Bobby Rouse had disappeared. "We might as well," she said. "I don't think we'll find Rouse now."

Kyle leaned forward and brushed a lock of hair off Bess's face. "Hey, are you okay?"

"I think so," Bess replied with a weak smile.

Twenty minutes later, the teens were back at Caroline Hill's busy headquarters.

"Chief McGinnis on the line for Nancy

Drew!" a dark-haired woman called out, holding up a phone.

Nancy hurried over and took the receiver from her. "Hi, Chief, what's up?"

"Nancy, we just stopped Bobby Rouse for speeding," the police chief told Nancy. "He was driving a stolen car. I just wanted to let you know he's in custody. If we turn up anything regarding Caroline Hill, I'll let you know."

Nancy told him about the hair-raising chase.

"We picked him up right near that construction site," the chief told her. "He was probably speeding in order to get away from you."

"I don't suppose I could get a look at the police report once your officers have questioned Rouse," Nancy said.

"It's against policy," Chief McGinnis said. There was a short pause, then he added, "But you've helped out the River Heights PD more than a few times in the past. Why don't you come down later, and I'll see what I can do."

After thanking the police chief, Nancy hung up. She relayed Chief McGinnis's news to Bess and Kyle, then said, "Come on. We'd better fill Caroline in on this."

When the three walked into Caroline's office, they found her pacing next to her desk as she talked on the phone.

"Mr. Davison," Caroline said patiently, "I know the photo looks real, but I assure you, the story is a lie. I would really hate to lose your

41

support based on such a slanderous article. . . . Yes, I'm doing all I can to find out who did it. . . . Great! Thank you for having confidence in me."

A moment later, Caroline hung up. "Hi. Did you find Bobby Rouse?"

"Well, yes and no," Bess replied. She, Nancy, and Kyle told Caroline about the car chase and the news of Bobby Rouse's arrest. "Chief McGinnis said he'd let us know if they learn anything about the fencing ring story," Nancy finished.

Caroline sighed and sat down at her desk. "I hope we get something concrete soon—before I start losing support."

"I know," Nancy said. "There's one other thing. Are you aware that Steve Hill is working for Gleason?"

"You mean my ex-husband?" Caroline asked in surprise.

Nancy nodded. "Ned heard that he was working for Gleason because he doesn't want his ex-wife for a boss."

"That sounds like Steve," Caroline said. "We were both in law school when we got married. Steve was going to be a tax attorney, but he dropped out and became an accountant. He's a really good one, too, but he was always jealous of me and my law career. It's what drove us apart after eight years of marriage—we've been divorced for two years now."

"Do you think he's vindictive enough to make up that fencing story and leak it to the press?" Bess asked.

Caroline shrugged. "He's bitter, but Steve is just a number cruncher. I can't picture him going to the trouble of staging such an elaborate hoax."

"Why is that?" Kyle asked.

"Caroline," Hector interrupted, sticking his head in the door, "we have to be across town to meet the teachers' union in fifteen minutes."

"Be right out," Caroline replied, then looked at Kyle. "Steve can be mean, but he never had the stomach for battle. I just can't believe he'd organize this whole thing. Let me know at the rally if you find out anything new." She grabbed her briefcase and hurried out the door.

Nancy had been so busy investigating, that she'd forgotten about the rally that night. "We'll be there!" she called after Caroline. After the candidate left, Nancy pulled her notebook from her shoulder bag and reached for the phone.

"Trying the other number again?" Bess asked.

Nancy nodded. This time, someone answered after the second ring.

"Hello?" said a woman's throaty voice.

Nancy's mind raced as she tried to think of a way to find out who the person was without arousing suspicion. "Um, hi, Vera, this is Sandy," Nancy chirped in a bright voice.

"Who?" the woman asked.

"Oh, I'm sorry. You aren't Vera Millhouse?" Nancy said. She noticed that Kyle and Bess were looking at her as if she were crazy.

The woman sounded annoyed as she said, "No, you must have the wrong number."

"This isn't the Millhouses' residence?" Nancy pressed.

"No," the woman snapped. "This is the home of Steve Hill. There is no Vera Millhouse at this number!" Then the woman hung up with a bang.

"All right!" Nancy shouted as she replaced the receiver in its cradle. "You guys, this number is for Steve Hill's house!"

"Really?" Bess said, her eyes widening. "Then he was probably the one who gave Brenda the photo!"

"It looks like it," Nancy replied.

"So now what do we do?" Kyle asked.

"First, I want to stop by the police station and look at Bobby Rouse's police report," Nancy said. "While I'm gone, could the two of you call Ned and find out if Steve Hill is working at Gleason's all afternoon? See if you can get Hill's address from Ned, too. I think it's time we checked out his house."

Kyle elbowed Bess lightly in the ribs. "Hey, this investigating stuff is pretty exciting," he said. "Especially when I'm working with you."

Bess's cheeks turned bright red. "Sherlock here is really eager to get on the case, Nan. You'd better hurry, or he'll go over to Steve Hill's without us!"

When Nancy arrived at the River Heights police headquarters, Chief McGinnis introduced her to one of the officers who had arrested Bobby Rouse, a blond-haired young man named Officer Denning.

"Well, it's not official policy, but seeing as you're a friend of Chief McGinnis, you can have a look at the report," he said, leading Nancy to a metal desk in the open room behind the receiving sergeant. He picked up a few typed pages from the desk and handed them to Nancy.

Still standing, she eagerly scanned the report. Rouse had been arrested at 1:45 P.M., just a few streets from the construction site. Nancy noted his home address, but she didn't see anything else that would help her.

"Have you questioned Rouse yet?" she asked.

"My partner's talking to him," Officer Denning told her. Glancing toward a set of glass doors at the rear of the room, he said, "In fact, there they are now."

Nancy looked over and saw Bobby Rouse being led through the doorway in handcuffs by a stout, balding police officer. "Hey, Pete, we need you in interrogation," the heavyset officer called to Officer Denning.

Nancy couldn't resist trying to talk to Rouse.

She walked toward him, but his face hardened when he saw her.

"You again!" Rouse exclaimed.

"Mr. Rouse, you know Caroline Hill wasn't involved in any fencing ring," Nancy said, ignoring the curious stares of Officer Denning and his partner. "Who paid you to pose in that photo?"

Rouse looked straight ahead and refused to meet her gaze. "Look, I'm not talking to any reporters."

Nancy blinked. He thought she was a reporter? So *that* was why he had taken off when she approached him at the diner. "I'm a detective, not a reporter. Who paid you to pose for that photograph? Was it Steve Hill?"

Nancy thought she saw Rouse's eyes shift nervously, but before he could say anything, Officer Denning's partner broke in. "Look, I'm sorry, miss," he said firmly. "Only his lawyer is allowed to talk to him. Come on, Pete."

With that, the officer led Bobby Rouse back down the hallway. "Sorry, but rules are rules," Officer Denning said. After taking the police report from Nancy, he followed his partner.

Another dead end, Nancy thought, letting out a sigh of frustration. She just hoped that Kyle, Bess, and she had better luck at Steve Hill's house later.

"Ned told us that Steve would be handing out Gleason pamphlets until seven or so," Bess told

Nancy a short while later. The two girls and Kyle were driving toward Steve Hill's neighborhood in Nancy's Mustang.

Nancy checked her watch. "Good, that gives us two hours," she said. A few minutes later, she pulled up next to the curb a safe distance from Steve Hill's modest split-level house.

"What are we looking for?" Kyle asked as they all got out of the car.

"Anything connecting him to that photograph or to the phony story about Caroline," Nancy said.

She started toward the house, then motioned for the others to stop. "Wait, a car's pulling out of his driveway!"

The three pretended to talk casually, but Nancy kept her eye on the big sedan. She caught a glimpse of a red-haired woman behind the wheel. As the woman drove away, Nancy noted her license plate number.

"I wonder if that's the woman you talked to on the phone?" Bess asked as Nancy scribbled down the number on her pad.

"Maybe," Nancy said, but she was already thinking ahead. "Bess, you'd better stay here as lookout while Kyle and I try to get into Hill's house."

Nervous, Bess looked up and down the street. "Okay, but hurry!"

After knocking on the door to make sure no one was home, Nancy said, "Let's try around back. I don't want anyone to see us breaking in the front door."

"Good idea," Kyle agreed.

Nancy led the way around the back and tried the door there, but it was locked.

"Now what?" Kyle asked.

Nancy was rummaging through her bag. "I've got my lock-picking kit with me."

"Wow," Kyle said. "You really *are* a pro."

Nancy smiled as she pulled out a narrow strip of metal. Suddenly she heard someone shout, "Stop!"

Nancy turned—and gasped. Kyle was struggling with someone!

The person had his back to Nancy, and all she saw was a glimpse of red hair. Then the man pushed Kyle away and whirled around to face Nancy. It was Steve Hill!

"You two are lucky I don't have a gun," he growled, "or you'd both be dead right now!"

Chapter

Six

NANCY FELT A CHILL pass from head to toe. What had happened to Bess? Nancy wondered.

"I ought to shoot you punks for trespassing," Steve said menacingly. He bent to pick up a bulging manila envelope that he'd dropped on the grass. "It's a good thing I was passing out these pamphlets in this neighborhood. If I hadn't decided to cut through my backyard to the next street, you'd be inside robbing me blind right now."

"Hey, we're not thieves!" Kyle said defensively.

Steve Hill looked dubiously from Nancy to Kyle and back to Nancy again. "Yeah, tell me about it."

Nancy decided to be direct. "Mr. Hill, I'm a detective, and my friends are helping me investi-

49

gate the allegations against Caroline Hill. We're here because we have reason to believe you're the one who gave the story to *Today's Times.*"

"What makes you think the story isn't true?" he demanded. "I gave that photograph and story to the newspaper because Caroline really *is* a criminal. I don't have to make up stories about her!"

"You mean you actually *believe* the story about the fencing ring?" Kyle asked.

Steve Hill nodded emphatically. "Since you're so sure the story is true," Nancy said, "then I'm sure you won't mind telling us who gave you that photograph."

"You're a nervy kid, aren't you?" Hill sneered. "It doesn't matter who it came from. All that matters is that Caroline be exposed for the lying crook she really is!"

Nancy pulled her copy of the article out of her shoulder bag and held it out to Steve Hill. "If the article is true, then how do you explain the missing bracelet in this photo?" she demanded. "Caroline never removes the medical ID bracelet she wears—you must know that. So why isn't the woman in the photograph wearing one?"

A glimmer of doubt crossed Hill's face as he stared at the grainy picture. "The quality of that photograph is terrible," he argued, but Nancy noticed that he didn't sound so sure of himself anymore. "It just doesn't show up."

He shoved the clipping back at Nancy. "Now,

why don't you two get out of here before I call the cops," he threatened. "And tell Caroline not to send any more of her juvenile delinquents around here again!"

Nancy and Kyle hurried back to the car, where they found Bess nervously pacing the sidewalk. "You guys, I'm so sorry! By the time I saw that red-haired man, he was already cutting through the yard to the back. I sneaked around to warn you, but he had already caught you. Was that Steve Hill?"

Kyle nodded. "Don't worry about it, Bess," he said, giving her arm a squeeze. "At least he didn't call the police."

As the three of them drove back toward the campaign headquarters, Kyle and Nancy told Bess about their confrontation with Steve Hill. "Someone else definitely fed him that story, but he wouldn't say who," Nancy explained.

Bess bit her lip. "So far Patrick Gleason is the only person we know with any motive to ruin Caroline's reputation. But I still can't believe he'd do that."

"I hope you're right, but we can't know for sure without concrete proof," Nancy said. "I'm glad the rally for Caroline is in a few hours. Right now, I could use a distraction from this case!"

"The speeches are going great," Bess whispered later Monday evening. She, Nancy, and Bess were standing at the rear of the River

Heights High School auditorium. The place was packed.

Several people had brought up the newspaper article, but Nancy thought Hector and Caroline had done a good job of handling the problem.

"I can assure you," Caroline was now saying, "that we will find out who is behind this vicious attack and win this race!"

As Caroline continued speaking, Nancy was glad to see the crowd's enthusiasm building. When the candidate finished, the entire auditorium erupted in cheers.

Nancy, Bess, and Kyle made their way to the front of the auditorium to talk to Caroline. When they got there, they found her surrounded by people. "Looks like she'll be busy for a while," Kyle said. "Let's get something to eat." He nodded toward one wall where a table of punch and snacks had been set up.

They were just finished eating some chips and dip when Caroline joined them. "What a nice turnout," she said, filling a glass with punch. "Did you make any progress finding out who planted the story?"

Nancy told Caroline about her visit to the police station and the confrontation with Steve Hill. "We still don't know who fed Steve the story, though," Nancy finished.

"It figures that he'd be willing to believe that trash about me," Caroline said. "Oh—I almost forgot to tell you. Someone from the DA's office called me just before the rally. Bobby Rouse is out on bail."

"Where did he get the money?" Bess asked.

Caroline shrugged. "Good question. It was a stiff bail, thirty thousand dollars. I have a theory, though. It's been my experience as a lawyer that the longer someone sits in jail, the more willing he is to talk."

"So you think someone might have sprung Rouse in order to keep him from talking?" Nancy asked.

"Maybe," Caroline replied. "Jerry! Thanks for coming," she said, turning to a man who tapped her on the shoulder. With an apologetic smile at Nancy, Caroline said, "We'll talk more tomorrow, okay?" Then she disappeared into the crowd.

Nancy turned to Bess and Kyle. "I want to find out who bailed out Bobby Rouse. It might be the person who got him to pose for that photo."

"We won't have much time tomorrow," Kyle told her. "I have to work at your dad's office, and you and Bess have to attend Caroline's speech in the park."

Nancy raised an eyebrow. "True, but there's always tonight," she said, glancing at her watch. "It's eight-thirty now."

Just then a guy wearing a gold lamé tuxedo and sunglasses sauntered past them. Kyle shaded his eyes and joked, "Man, I can't see! That suit is blinding me!"

"I almost forgot about the entertainment part of this rally," Bess said, giggling. "Let's at least listen to the band before we go check out Bobby Rouse, okay?"

"Sounds good," Nancy agreed. When the group of guys started to play, she couldn't help moving to the beat. Pretty soon a large group of Caroline Hill supporters were dancing on the stage. During a fast song, Nancy almost knocked into someone at the edge of the crowd. Turning, she saw that it was Brenda Carlton.

"Oops, sorry, Brenda," Nancy said breathlessly, coming to a stop. "What brings you here? Don't tell me you're a Hill supporter."

"Hardly!" Brenda replied sourly, holding up her reporter's pad. "I happen to be working on an assignment, thanks to you."

"How's that?" Nancy asked.

Brenda put a hand on her hip. "After you talked to my father about my article, he had no choice but to ask me to write a retraction to the Caroline Hill scandal if I couldn't verify positively that the photo was accurate and not doctored. I just got a statement from Ms. Hill."

Before Nancy could reply, Bess and Kyle came up to her. "Hey, Nan, it's almost nine. Maybe we'd better go look for Bobby Rouse now and—" Bess broke off when she saw Brenda.

"Bobby Rouse?" Brenda was suddenly alert. "What are you going to talk to him about?"

Bess shot Nancy an apologetic look. "It's nothing, Brenda, really," Bess said, but the reporter didn't look convinced.

"You guys are up to something." Brenda closed her notebook. "I'm coming with you. Don't even try to talk me out of it," she said firmly. "I have as much of a right to talk to him as you do."

"Look, Brenda—" Nancy began.

"Either you let me come with you, or I follow you, anyway," Brenda said.

Nancy exchanged a look with Bess and Kyle. At least if Brenda was with them, Nancy thought, they might be able to keep her from doing something stupid. "Well, okay," Nancy finally said. "But first I want to make a few calls. I'll meet you all at my car in a couple of minutes."

While the others headed outside, Nancy found a pay phone in the lobby and called Chief McGinnis. "Hi, Chief," she said when he came on the line. "I heard that Bobby Rouse is out on bail. Can you tell me who posted the bond?"

She waited while he called for the report. "A guy named Ralph Lemko," Chief McGinnis said.

"Hmm. That could be the same Ralph I saw Rouse talking to earlier today," Nancy said.

Chief McGinnis gave her Lemko's address. "Oh, one more thing," he told her. "I ran a computer check on Bobby Rouse. It turns out that the address he gave us is false. I thought you'd want to know, in case you're planning on talking to him."

Nancy tried to hide her disappointment.

"Thanks for letting me know," she said. "I guess I'll have to try to find him somewhere else."

After hanging up, Nancy joined Kyle, Bess, and Brenda at her car. They piled in, with Bess and Kyle in the backseat and Brenda up front with Nancy.

"The address we have for Bobby Rouse is bogus, so let's drive by Slim and Shorty's," Nancy suggested as they drove away. "Maybe we'll find Rouse or his friend Ralph."

When they reached the diner, Nancy slowed down to look around. The lights at Slim and Shorty's glowed brightly, but just about every other building around was dark.

"This neighborhood looks even scarier at night than it did this morning," Bess said with a shiver.

Nancy pulled to a halt in front of the diner and gazed through the windows that ran the full length of the front. The diner was almost deserted. The booths were empty. An old man sat over his coffee at a long counter, and a short, fat cook in a dirty apron read the paper.

"I don't see either Rouse or his friend in there," Kyle said, frowning. "Now what?"

"I can't believe you guys made me go on a total wild-goose chase!" Brenda sighed in exasperation.

"What a drag," Nancy muttered. She pulled into the street, then turned into an alley to turn around. Her headlights lit up a parked car about halfway down the narrow drive.

"Better back out, Nan," Bess advised.

"Wait," Nancy said, peering ahead. "Why is the passenger door on that car open?"

"Who cares?" Brenda said. "It's an abandoned car. Let's just get out of here."

But Nancy was already out of the car. Kyle and Bess followed, with Brenda trailing behind. Nancy couldn't see anyone in the rust-pitted sedan as she approached, but that didn't mean that the driver wasn't in or near the car. She looked in all directions, then peered through the open door.

The next instant, Nancy gasped and jerked back. Stretched out on the front seat was Bobby Rouse. He was staring up at her with dead, unseeing eyes.

Nancy felt a wave of nausea as she leaned in for a closer look. Bobby's expression was frozen in a look of mild surprise, his eyes blank. Blood still trickled from a neat, round bullet hole above his ear.

Behind her, Nancy heard Bess and Brenda muffle screams.

"Is he dead?" Kyle asked, hugging Bess to his chest.

Nancy reached in and gingerly felt Rouse's pulse, then gave a terse nod.

"I think I feel sick," Brenda said in a tight voice. "I have to get out of here. I mean, I, uh, better go back and call in to the newspaper with this right away." She took off down the alley.

"Call the police, too!" Nancy called after her.

Nancy's gaze ran over the car's interior, which was empty except for a takeout coffee container and a scrap of paper lying on the dashboard. Leaning over, she read aloud the words scrawled on the paper: " 'Nine o'clock, Greenwood.' "

Kyle checked his watch. "It's nearly ten o'clock," he said. "Do you think that note's about some kind of meeting?"

"Maybe," Nancy replied. "But I wonder what or who Greenwood is? And if Greenwood has anything to do with why he was killed." She turned and headed toward the alley's entrance. "Come on, let's go make sure Brenda called the police."

"What did Caroline say when you told her about Bobby Rouse?" Bess whispered to Nancy Tuesday morning.

Nancy had just taken a seat next to her friend in the front row of folding chairs set up in the middle of Farragut Park, near downtown River Heights. Caroline, standing on a platform decorated with red, white, and blue bunting, was about to speak to a coalition of teens and senior citizens who had banded together to clean up the park.

"She was pretty upset," Nancy answered. "Not only is she being framed, but someone's actually been killed. And now Bobby Rouse can never tell us who arranged for him to pose in that photograph."

"Which means that Caroline might never find out who's trying to ruin her campaign," Bess finished.

Turning around in her chair, Nancy glanced at the crowd. Her gaze narrowed when she saw three college-aged guys standing in the back.

"Bess!" she said softly, pointing. "I saw those guys at Patrick Gleason's headquarters yesterday. They were bad-mouthing Caroline."

Bess frowned. "What are they doing here?"

"Beats me, but I'm going to keep an eye on them." Nancy turned back to face front as Caroline was introduced to the crowd.

"Friends," Caroline began, "I remember just two years ago when this park was a wasteland where children never played and people were afraid to walk at night. But through your hard, unselfish work—"

"Murderer!" a voice shouted from the back row, cutting Caroline short.

Turning around, Nancy saw that the three guys from Gleason's office were on their feet. Now they all shouted together, "Murderer!" One guy was holding up a sign in dripping red paint: The Answer: Hill Killed Rouse.

Nancy gasped and jumped to her feet. "Bess, we have to get them out of here right away! This could ruin Caroline's campaign!"

She had only gone a step when the three young men rushed up to the dais.

"They have something under their shirts!"

59

Bess said, gripping Nancy's arm. "They're going to hurt Caroline!"

Nancy sprinted toward the guys, but it was too late.

"No! Don't do it!" Caroline shouted as one of the men heaved a small, round object at her. It was a balloon, Nancy realized.

Nancy froze as she saw the balloon strike Caroline and explode. The next instant, Caroline was covered head to toe in blood!

Chapter

Seven

NANCY WATCHED IN HORROR as Caroline staggered backward, dazed, dripping with the gooey red liquid.

"You'll never get Bobby Rouse's blood off your hands, Hill!" a wiry member of the trio snarled.

Nancy leapt into action, covering the last few steps to Caroline. Bess was right behind her. Catching Caroline by the shoulders, Nancy and Bess turned her away from the hecklers.

"It's paint," Nancy told Caroline as soon as she saw the red liquid up close.

Hector and several volunteers sprinted up from their chairs and tackled two of the attackers, while the third got away. The whole crowd was in an uproar.

All at once Caroline seemed to recover from the shock. "This has to stop!" she said angrily.

THE NANCY DREW FILES

She strode over to the two men who were pinned to the ground. Nancy and Bess followed.

"What is the meaning of this outrage!" Caroline demanded.

The two men got to their feet. Nancy saw the beefy guy's Adam's apple bob as he looked at Caroline. "You know what it's about!" he shot back. "It's all over the front page of *Today's Times*. Bobby Rouse was found murdered last night."

"We know you killed him," the wiry one broke in. "Why don't you just give up now?"

"Uh-oh," Nancy whispered in Bess's ear. "This kind of publicity is really going to hurt Caroline."

"That's just what these guys want," Bess said, shaking her head in disgust.

"Caroline," Nancy said, stepping forward, "I think you should know that these guys work on Patrick Gleason's campaign."

Turning back to the young men, Caroline demanded, "Does Patrick Gleason know anything about this?"

"He had nothing to do with this," the thin one replied. "We were acting on our own."

Caroline's questioning was interrupted when two police officers showed up to take the protesters away. Caroline regained her composure. Before she returned to the dais, she said to Nancy, "I'm going to have to change clothes after this, but I'd like you to meet me back at headquarters later to fill me in on any new developments."

While Caroline tried to calm the crowd, Bess whispered, "What are we going to do to stop all these lies, Nancy?"

"We have to find out who planted that story about Caroline and who killed Bobby Rouse and why," she said. "Right now Steve Hill and Patrick Gleason are our only suspects. I'm meeting Ned for lunch later. Maybe he can help me find out what, if anything, either Gleason or Steve Hill knows about Bobby Rouse's death."

"And about that Greenwood thing in the note we found in Rouse's car," Bess added.

Nancy nodded. "Right. Caroline and Patrick Gleason are going to be debating this afternoon at four. Maybe Ned can help me check out Gleason's office for clues then, while everyone is at the debate. But for now, why don't you and I wait for Caroline at her headquarters?"

Nancy dug her notebook out of her shoulder bag and ripped out one of the pages. "This is the license plate number of the woman we saw at Hill's house yesterday," she said, handing Bess the paper. "It's a long shot, but maybe the woman fits into Caroline's frame-up or Bobby Rouse's murder somehow. While we're waiting for Caroline, we can call the Department of Motor Vehicles and try to trace the plate and find out the owner's name."

"Shouldn't we be looking into Greenwood, too?" Bess asked.

"Definitely. We can search the phone book for every Greenwood in the area."

An hour later Caroline returned to the campaign office. Leaving Bess poring over the phone book for any Greenwoods, Nancy went into the back office to talk to the candidate. She spotted a copy of *Today's Times* on Caroline's desk. "Oh, so here's the article on Bobby Rouse's murder," Nancy said to Caroline as she picked up the paper.

Skimming through the article, Nancy was relieved to see that there was nothing linking the murder to Caroline. In a small box at the bottom of the page, a few lines mentioned that there had been some "factual errors" in the previous day's article about the fencing ring, as well as a short quote from Caroline.

"It's not much of an apology," Nancy said, folding up the paper in disgust.

Caroline simply nodded as she sat behind her desk. "After this morning, I have other things to worry about. Hector has talked to Patrick Gleason's manager about the incident in Farragut Park," she said. "He told Hector that the attackers have already been fired. Gleason is issuing a statement condemning the attack, too. But I'm afraid those hecklers' claims will still hurt my campaign.

"I'm also concerned that you could be in danger. If Rouse's murder is related to my being framed, that means someone is willing to kill to make sure I'm not elected. He might hurt you, too, Nancy."

A knock on the door made them look up. Bess was standing in the doorway. "Nan," Bess said, "I'm still working on Greenwood, but I did find out who owns the car we saw at Steve's house. It's someone named Anna Dimitros."

"Anna Dimitros!" Caroline burst out, sitting forward. "Are you sure?"

Bess nodded. "Positive. Why? Who is she?"

"The former owner and president of Helen of Troy Cosmetics," Caroline explained. "She was charged with manslaughter when three of the workers in her manufacturing plant died after they were exposed to lethal doses of formaldehyde. That plant was one of the most dangerous workplaces I've ever seen. I prosecuted Dimitros, and I won. She got a five-year prison term, and her business went bankrupt. She must have gotten out on parole recently."

Nancy let out a low whistle. "So basically her whole life went down the tubes. Is she the kind of person who would try to get back at you?"

"And why would she be at your ex-husband's house?" Bess added. "Unless they're *both* plotting to frame you."

"Why not?" Nancy said, growing excited. "We should definitely check out Anna Dimitros, that's

65

for sure." She glanced at her watch and frowned. "I have to meet Ned for lunch now, but maybe you could do some checking, Bess."

"Anything," Bess said, grinning. "Kyle should be here soon, too, so he can help me."

"Maybe you two could go to the library and look up back articles about Dimitros's trial. Make copies of anything you find, okay? And see if you can find out any connection between her and Greenwood, too."

"No problem!" Bess sang.

Ned was answering phones when Nancy walked into Gleason's headquarters a half-hour later. He waved at her and signaled that he'd be off in a few minutes.

Trying to act casual, Nancy glanced around the room. She didn't see Gleason, but Steve Hill jumped up from a table as soon as he saw her.

"What do you think you're doing here?" he snapped, stopping inches from her face.

"I'm here to meet my boyfriend, Ned, for lunch," she replied evenly. "And to find out what you think about Bobby Rouse's murder."

"I never met the guy," Steve told her. "Why would I think anything about it?"

Nancy decided to try a different tack. "What about Greenwood?" she asked. "Does that name mean anything to you?"

Steve Hill shook a finger in her face. "Look, even if I knew anything about this Greenwood, I wouldn't tell you." His voice dropped to a menacing growl. "But I will tell you that you'd better watch out. All your snooping could get you into deep trouble!" With that, he turned and stalked off.

Nancy was still staring after Steve Hill when Ned came up behind her and gave her a quick hug. "Have you been harassing the enemy?" he asked jokingly.

"We've been harassing each other," Nancy told him. "Let's go eat. I'm starved!"

As Ned and Nancy walked down the block to a pizza place, they discussed the paint-throwing incident.

"Gleason held a staff meeting to condemn the attack," Ned said, after they had settled into a booth and ordered.

"Great, but that makes it harder for me to ask you to do me a big favor," Nancy said.

"Try me," Ned said. He looked up as the waitress delivered their pizza, then picked up a slice.

Nancy took a deep breath. "I want you to help me search Patrick Gleason's office this afternoon, during the debate. I have to find out if there's anything about the frame-up in Gleason's papers."

"You still think that Gleason might have something to do with that?" Ned asked, studying her. When Nancy nodded, he took a huge breath and let it out slowly.

"Okay, I'll do it," he finally said. "But only because I want Gleason's name cleared. I'll try to fix it so I'm the only one there during the debate."

"Thanks, Ned," Nancy said, reaching over the table to squeeze his hand.

After they had finished eating, Nancy left Ned at Gleason's campaign office and returned to Caroline Hill's headquarters. She found Bess and Kyle sitting at a table covered with photocopies and containers of Mexican food.

"Hi, Nan!" Bess called out, biting into a tortilla chip.

"Here, Nancy, try a nacho," Kyle chimed in, handing her a chip dripping with cheese. "These are the best in the universe."

Nancy popped it into her mouth. "Not bad," she admitted. "Any luck at the library?"

Bess handed Nancy a photocopied newspaper article. "We struck out with Greenwood, but we did find this."

"It's an article that came out the day after Anna Dimitros was found guilty of manslaughter," Kyle explained. "Read the part that's highlighted."

Nancy skimmed down to the paragraph outlined in yellow. "'A hostile crowd followed Dimitros and her laywers out of the courthouse and surrounded her as she got into a waiting limousine,'" she read aloud. "'Responding to their taunts, Dimitros stated in a ringing voice,

"I have done nothing wrong. Caroline Hill is the one who should be ashamed. Someday, she will have to pay a price for ruining my life.'''"

"Wow!" Nancy exclaimed, setting the article down. "Anna Dimitros blames everything on Caroline. The question is, what sort of price does she want Caroline to pay?"

"I'll bet anything that Anna Dimitros is getting her revenge by framing Caroline Hill!" Bess exclaimed.

Chapter

Eight

KYLE WHISTLED SOFTLY. "In a sick way, it makes sense that Dimitros would try to get back at Caroline this way."

"Maybe Anna Dimitros figured that since Caroline destroyed her career, her best revenge would be to ruin *Caroline's* career."

"But I still don't get how Dimitros could know Steve Hill," Kyle said. "Or how she knew Bobby Rouse."

Nancy shrugged. "We'll definitely have to do more investigating. But if Anna Dimitros was willing to let people die in her factory, maybe she was willing to kill Bobby Rouse to keep him from spilling the beans about her being responsible for the story framing Caroline."

The conversation was interrupted by a door

slamming shut. They looked up to see Hector stomping out of Caroline's office.

"Hector, what is it?" Nancy asked.

"I've been trying to get through to Sam Filanowski to ask him if he'll speak out against these attacks on Caroline," Hector replied. "He won't even give me the time of day. I'm starting to think that what people are saying is true."

"What's that?" Bess asked, dabbing at a spot of hot sauce on her shirt.

"I guess you didn't read the editorial page of the *Morning Record*," he said. "One columnist commented on how strange it was that the mayor isn't supporting Caroline when in the past he's always sung her praises. The article said that by not supporting her, Filanowski is actually telling people they should vote for Gleason."

"But that's crazy!" Bess exclaimed. "The mayor isn't supporting Gleason, either."

"But the mayor doesn't really know Gleason," Hector explained. "Everyone assumed that Filanowski would come out for Caroline."

Nancy frowned. "Why would he turn his back on her?"

"I'm not sure." Hector threw up his hands. "A year or so ago, he lost a lot of money in a risky real estate deal, and Caroline was one of the only people he told. But since his heart attack several months ago, he's become more and more distant. Now he won't even talk to her on the phone!"

"I wish we could just walk right into Filanowski's office and ask him what the deal is," Kyle remarked.

Bess shook her head as she started collecting the food wrappers on the table. "It makes me sick that Brenda Carlton is the only person the mayor will talk to."

Nancy stared at her friend. "That's it! Bess, you're a genius!"

"I am?" Bess asked, looking up in surprise.

"Yes," Nancy replied, grinning. "I'd forgotten all about Brenda's interview. Maybe there's a way we can make it work for us. Hector, what's Mayor Filanowski's office number?"

Hector, Bess, and Kyle gathered around as Nancy dialed the number Hector gave her. When the mayor's secretary answered, Nancy tried to make her voice sound like Brenda's. "Hello, this is Brenda Carlton, of *Today's Times.*" In a teary voice, she explained that she'd made a horrible scheduling mistake and would it be possible to interview the mayor the following day instead of Friday? If not, she'd miss her deadline and lose her job. To Nancy's relief, the secretary bought her story. She rescheduled the interview for the next morning.

"Talk about sneaky," Kyle said with a big grin. "I love it!"

"Way to go!" Hector shook Nancy's shoulder. "Maybe you can convince Filanowski to help Caroline out a little."

"I hope so," Nancy told him. "In the meantime, I'm going to be busy. First, I want to go to Anna Dimitros's and see what I can find out. And if there's time before the debate, I'd like to take another crack at getting into Steve Hill's house to look for evidence there."

After checking his watch, Kyle said apologetically, "Sorry, but I'll have to pass. I'd hoped to be able to spend all afternoon here, but I could only get away for a long lunch hour. Your dad needs me to do some research, Nancy."

"But you can count me in," Bess said brightly. "Let's go!"

The information Bess had gotten from the Motor Vehicle Department listed Anna Dimitros's address in a slightly run-down neighborhood on the outskirts of River Heights. Nancy had called ahead, pretending to be a journalist for the high school paper. When she told Anna Dimitros that she and Bess were doing an article about local businesswomen, Dimitros had readily agreed to talk to them.

It was just before two when Nancy pulled her Mustang up in front of the brick apartment building, and she and Bess got out and looked around.

"Yuck!" Bess exclaimed as she stepped around an overflowing garbage can on the sidewalk.

"My sentiments exactly," Nancy said, walking up to the front door. The building had no elevator, and she and Bess were breathless by the time they climbed the five flights of stairs and knocked on Anna Dimitros's door.

"Those stairs will be the death of me," Anna Dimitros greeted the girls. An unlit cigarette in hand, she waved them into the narrow hallway. In her late forties, Anna wore heavy makeup, and her hair was dyed an unnatural shade of red. Still, Nancy thought that she was a striking woman. She swept ahead of Nancy and Bess in her flowing silk kimono and led them into a tiny living room furnished with a couch, a chair, two end tables, and a typewriter on a small table.

"Please excuse my living quarters," Anna said, lighting her cigarette and settling back into a chair. "But it *is* an improvement over cell block A." She threw back her head and gave a short, throaty laugh.

Nancy and Bess sat down on the sagging sofa.

"How exactly can I help you two lovely girls?" Anna went on, exhaling a thick stream of smoke.

"Well, Bess and I are writing a series about local businesswomen," Nancy began. "We'd like to hear about how you built up your successful cosmetics company."

"We both have *loads* of admiration for you," Bess gushed, beaming.

Anna narrowed her black-rimmed eyes at them. "You do know how I lost my company, don't you?" Without waiting for an answer, she said, "That Hill woman ruined my reputation, destroyed my business, and wrecked my life all in the name of ruthless ambition! Bringing down a powerful person like me was a real feather in her cap, you know."

"Are you talking about Caroline Hill, the mayoral candidate?" Bess asked with wide, innocent eyes.

"The mayoral candidate," Anna repeated disdainfully. "What a joke! Let me tell you, I know some things about Caroline Hill that the public doesn't."

"You mean like the fencing ring story?" Nancy asked.

Anna waved her cigarette dismissively. "That's nothing. I know worse secrets about Caroline Hill."

Bess exchanged a quick look with Nancy, then leaned toward Anna and asked, "Like what?"

"No, no, no!" Anna replied coyly. "That will have to wait. You see, I, too, am a writer." She pointed to the typewriter set up in the corner of the room. "I began working on a nonfiction book while I was in prison, and now I'm writing the final draft, with the help of a dear friend."

Nancy wasn't sure what this might have to do with her case, but she decided to find out all she could. "Oh? And who is helping you?"

"He's Steve Hill, Caroline's ex-husband," Anna said, her voice softening for the first time. "I wanted some information on his wife, and I asked him if he'd be willing to be interviewed.

We became friends, and our friendship has blossomed into a wonderful romance."

So maybe Dimitros and Steve Hill *were* working together, Nancy thought.

"That's so cool!" Bess breathed. "And you're a real writer! Would you mind showing me around? I'd love to see how a writer lives."

Nancy flashed Bess a congratulatory smile as Anna stood up. Now Nancy had a chance to look at Anna's notes by the typewriter. "Um, if you don't mind, I'll stay here. I want to write down all you've told us before I forget."

Nancy took out her notebook, but she put it aside as soon as Anna led Bess out of the living room. Nancy hurried over to the typewriter and shuffled through the notes stacked on and around it.

"Hmm, what's this?" Nancy murmured, thumbing through a stack of notecards. She paused at one card. It was a list of names and phone numbers. Next to some of them, Anna had written the word "interviewed" and a date. Steve Hill had been interviewed a few months earlier, Nancy noted as she ran her finger down the list.

Farther down, Nancy stopped again. Bobby Rouse was on the list! Anna had talked to him just one month earlier. So there *was* a connection between Rouse and Anna Dimitros. Hearing Anna's voice drifting toward the living room, Nancy quickly returned the card to the stack. She rushed back to the couch just a second before Anna and Bess reentered the room.

"Gosh, Bess, it's after two-thirty!" Nancy exclaimed, jumping up. "I just realized that we're late for our next interview." She put out her hand for Anna to shake. "Thanks for being so generous with your time, Ms. Dimitros."

Anna seemed disappointed that they were leaving so soon. "But I haven't had a chance to talk about my start in business," she protested.

The girls promised to call again, then left. Back in the car, Nancy told Bess about the notecard listing Steve Hill and Bobby Rouse.

"Wow. So if Dimitros knew Rouse, she could have hired him to pose for the photograph," Bess said as Nancy pulled out into traffic. "Maybe she even killed him!"

"We still don't know for sure," Nancy said. "But maybe we'll find more evidence at Steve Hill's house."

Bess shot Nancy a worried glance. "Nan, how are we going to get into his house without getting caught this time?"

"Ned told me that Mr. Hill is working in Patrick Gleason's campaign office all day," Nancy explained. "Then he's going to the debate. We'll just have to be careful that none of the neighbors see us."

Fifteen minutes later, the two girls were in Steve Hill's yard, checking his windows.

"Everything's locked up tight," Nancy said, yanking on the back door of the house. "I'll have to pick the lock."

After taking a narrow metal instrument from her shoulder bag, she inserted it into the keyhole. A few moments later, the lock clicked open.

"I keep expecting someone to jump out of the bushes," Bess said nervously, glancing around. "Let's get inside fast."

Nancy opened the door and stepped into a small room that held a washer and dryer. With Bess right behind her, she quietly walked through the laundry room and into the dimly lit kitchen.

Suddenly she cocked her head to one side. From far off in the house, she heard a faint scrabbling sound.

"What's that?" Bess asked behind her.

A split second later, a black Doberman came through the kitchen doorway. The dog let out a terrifying, deep-chested growl. Nancy's heart seemed to leap into her throat.

In the next instant, the Doberman ran straight at Bess and Nancy, his sharp white teeth bared.

"He's going to kill us!" Bess screamed.

Chapter

Nine

NANCY FROZE as the dog ran across the kitchen floor.

With the dog just a few feet away, Nancy forced herself to move. She whipped off her denim jacket and threw it at the dog, covering his head. Before the dog could shake the jacket off, she jumped forward to hold him still.

"Quick, Bess!" she said urgently. "Help me get him into the laundry room."

Bess's eyes were wide with fear as she jumped behind the dog and pushed on his haunches, while Nancy pulled him through the doorway. The Doberman locked his legs and tried to buck out of their grasp, his furious snarls barely muffled by the jacket. When they got him just inside the laundry room, Nancy took her jacket, and she and Bess jumped backward through the doorway, then slammed the door shut. A second later, they heard the dog jump at the door, barking with fury.

Bess shuddered. "I can't believe I just did that," she breathed, leaning against the kitchen wall.

"Me, either," Nancy replied as she sank into a chair at the round kitchen table. "I had no idea Mr. Hill had a dog."

Bess took a few deep breaths. "I guess we'd better start looking around before a neighbor hears that barking and decides to call the cops!"

"Good idea," Nancy said. "I'll search down-stairs, and you check the bedrooms."

"Find anything?" Bess asked a half hour later, joining Nancy in the den.

Nancy held up some press clippings she'd found on the desk. "Just these. They're articles about Caroline's run for mayor. But I haven't found anything linking Steve Hill to the frame-up."

"I couldn't find anything, either," Bess said, letting out a sigh of frustration. "I can't believe we've hit another dead end."

Checking her watch, Nancy said, "Yikes, the debate's starting in just fifteen minutes! I'll drop you off there, then call Ned to make sure he's the only one at Gleason's office. We'd better get going."

After leaving by the front door, the two girls drove across town to the River Heights cultural center, where the debate was being held. Bess went into the auditorium, while Nancy phoned Ned from the lobby.

"The coast is almost clear," Ned told her over the phone. "The last person is about to leave—I convinced her that I could handle the phones so she could watch the debate. I'll be the only one here."

"Great," Nancy said. "I'll be right over."

She hung up the phone and started for the door, walking past groups of River Heights residents who were arriving for the debate. She had only gone a few steps when she recognized a short, distinguished-looking man with graying blond hair standing by the auditorium doors. It was Alan Blount, Nancy realized, the man who had given Caroline the huge donation at her fundraiser Sunday night.

Nancy paused as Patrick Gleason, surrounded by a small group, entered the lobby. He smiled and waved at people he passed. When he got to the auditorium doorway, he reached out to shake hands with Alan Blount.

Don't bother trying to get Blount's support, Nancy thought. Then she saw Alan Blount lean toward Gleason and mutter under his breath, "Knock 'em dead, Pat!"

Nancy was stunned. What was Alan Blount doing encouraging Gleason, when he had donated so much money to Caroline's campaign? Had the fencing ring scandal made him switch sides?

Nancy shook her head and hurried out the door. She didn't have time to think about that now.

It was ten minutes after four when she arrived at Patrick Gleason's headquarters, where Ned was alone. He gave her a big smile, but Nancy thought she saw a glint of unease in his eyes.

"How's the case going?" he asked.

Nancy quickly filled him in on her interview with Anna Dimitros and the search of Steve Hill's house. "We still don't have proof linking anyone to the frame-up, though. Or to Bobby Rouse's murder."

"Well, let's get this over with." With a quick look to the door, Ned led the way to Gleason's office. Nancy glanced at the messy desk, shelves, and filing cabinets, then spun through the Rolodex on the candidate's desk. She didn't see any number for Bobby Rouse or for the mysterious "Greenwood" she'd seen on the note in Rouse's car. There was no card for Anna Dimitros or Steve Hill, either.

"I don't like lying, you know," Ned grumbled, yanking open a file drawer.

Nancy looked up at Ned in surprise. "Ned, what are you talking about?"

Ned pulled out a stack of files and leafed through them. "After you left here today, Steve

Hill told Gleason that you were snooping around for Caroline Hill, and about you and Kyle trying to break into his house. Then Gleason came to me and asked me what exactly you were up to, and if I was working for you. I told him that I backed him one hundred percent and that you and I kept your detective work out of our relationship."

Ned had kept his eyes focused on the files while he spoke. Then he jammed the files back in the drawer and pulled out another stack.

"I'm sorry about putting you in the middle of this, Ned, but it's important to get at the truth. Did Gleason seem nervous, like he might be afraid of what I'd find out?"

"You don't let up, do you!" Ned burst out, slamming the file drawer shut. "Patrick Gleason trusted me enough to leave me here alone today, and look what I'm doing—ransacking his private office, looking for evidence to use against him!"

Nancy wished she could get him to understand. "Ned, you're helping to find out who Rouse's killer is and who framed Caroline Hill. Gleason is a suspect, and the sooner we can investigate him the sooner he'll be cleared." If he's innocent, she added to herself. She knelt down to look in the bottom drawer.

"And in the meantime, it doesn't matter to you if Gleason finds out I've been spying on him and loses all respect for me," Ned said quietly.

Sitting back on her heels, Nancy looked up at

her boyfriend. "Oh, Ned, I'm so sorry," she apologized. "I wasn't thinking about that."

"Look, I'm sorry, too. I shouldn't have blown up at you," Ned said. "I know you have to investigate. It's just that I hate feeling like such a sneak."

Nancy got to her feet and gave him a quick hug. She was about to tell him that she understood, when her gaze landed on Gleason's typewriter.

"Hey, what's this?" She bent over a paper that was in the typewriter on a stand by the desk. It was a letter that Patrick Gleason was writing to *Today's Times,* criticizing them for printing the story about Caroline Hill.

"'Every American deserves a fair chance,'" Ned read out loud over Nancy's shoulder. "'And Caroline Hill hasn't been getting that, thanks to your story. I firmly believe that I am the best candidate for mayor, but I also believe that I should be given the chance to beat my opponent fair and square.'"

"What do you think of that?" Ned challenged.

Nancy nodded. "It's a good letter. Sounds sincere." She didn't add that Patrick Gleason might have written the letter just to throw suspicion off himself. She didn't want to start another fight with Ned. Then again, maybe Ned was right. They certainly hadn't found anything suspicious about Gleason so far.

Deep in thought, Nancy was tugging on a

stubborn desk drawer when suddenly the whole drawer popped out, and papers and pencils flew everywhere.

"Good work, Drew," Nancy scolded herself.

Ned started to laugh, then suddenly froze. "Shh! Someone's unlocking the outside door!"

Nancy heard the sound of a key turning in the lock. She looked at Ned in shock. How were they going to explain what they were doing in there—especially with half of Gleason's desk spilled all over the floor!

Ned quietly pushed the office door closed. A split second later, Nancy heard the front door swing open and heavy footsteps on the floor. The footsteps were getting closer.

Nancy looked at Ned and gulped. They were about to get caught red-handed!

Chapter

Ten

NANCY GLANCED frantically around the room. She had to think of a way to get them out of this mess—fast!

Suddenly she had an idea. Planting her hands on her hips, she faced her boyfriend and said in a loud, angry voice, "Ned Nickerson! You're a real jerk, you know that?"

Ned looked at her in astonishment. "What?" he said.

"Pretend we're fighting," she whispered, pointing to the door. Raising her voice to a shout, she said, "First, you tell me you don't even know the girl, and then you tell me she's just a friend!"

Nancy waved her hand at him to respond. Then she hurriedly bent down to pick up the contents of the drawer.

"Well, she *is* just a friend!" he defended himself loudly. Stifling a laugh, he helped Nancy return pens and papers to the drawer.

"Really?" Nancy's voice was icy as she scooped up paper clips. "And are you in the habit of kissing all your friends?"

They paused and listened: The footsteps had stopped. Good! Nancy thought. Hopefully the person was totally embarrassed and wondering what to do.

"You know, Nancy," Ned went on, "I'm getting really sick of your crazy accusations!" He finished putting the last of the items back in the drawer, then slid it into its slot.

"Is that so?" Nancy shot back. "Then maybe I should just leave right now!" She stormed out of the office and slammed the door behind her.

Their one-man audience, a tall, middle-aged man, was hovering near the office door when Nancy came out. She saw his face switch from fascination to embarrassment at being caught eavesdropping. Nancy faked a gasp of shock at his presence and hurried out the front door. Moments later, after apologizing to the staff member, Ned joined Nancy down the street, where they couldn't be seen from the headquarters' windows.

"Fights are fun when you don't mean it," Ned joked. He pulled Nancy into his arms as he leaned against a parked car.

"Aren't they, though?" Nancy agreed, wrapping her arms around his waist. "Maybe we should take up acting. We sure had that poor guy convinced!"

Ned laughed. "Yeah, that was Dave Mitchell, a staff member. I told him I was really sorry for using Gleason's office for our fight. I acted as embarrassed as he was." He kissed her hair.

"Hey," Nancy said, looking up into his face. She thought he looked cuter than ever. "How about dinner at my house tonight? I really owe you after all the trouble I keep getting you into. Hannah's making roast chicken and blueberry cobbler."

Ned grinned at her. "You're on. For tonight, you and I are going to forget about this campaign *and* your case."

He bent to kiss her, and Nancy found that she didn't have any problem forgetting about everything else in the world but Ned.

"Now, I'm supposed to be Molly Thomas, a photographer at *Today's Times,* right?" Bess asked Wednesday morning, as she and Nancy climbed the marble staircase in City Hall.

"That's right," Nancy replied. It was just before nine, the time of the appointment she had made with Mayor Filanowski, pretending to be Brenda. The girls' heels clicked across the polished hallway as they headed for the mayor's second-floor office. Bess was carrying a camera bag. "I can't believe Hector is trusting me with his best camera," she said. "I hope I don't drop it."

As they passed a mirror set in a gilt frame on the wall, Nancy paused to check her reflection. Staring back at her was a chic, sophisticated young woman, wearing a tailored houndstooth suit with a short, narrow skirt and black pumps.

"You look very Brenda Carlton," Bess said, giggling. "Especially with that red lipstick and French braid."

"I just hope he's never met Brenda before—or that it's so long ago that he's forgotten how she looks."

When the girls reached the mayor's office, Nancy introduced herself and Bess to the mayor's secretary, Mrs. Wellborn. The petite, gray-haired woman reminded Nancy of a small bird.

Pressing her intercom button, Mrs. Wellborn said, "Mayor, the Carlton girl is here for her interview, along with her photographer, Miss Thomas."

A moment later, a portly man in his early sixties appeared. "Come on in, Miss Carlton, Miss Thomas!"

Nancy had never met Mayor Filanowski before, but she recognized him from pictures she'd seen in the paper. He smiled jovially at the girls as he shook hands and waved them into his office.

Nancy exchanged a relieved look with Bess. Filanowski didn't seem to know that Nancy wasn't Brenda. So far so good!

The girls glanced around at the gleaming wood paneling and thick damask curtains, then sat in the upholstered chairs the mayor indicated by his desk. He sank into his leather desk chair and locked his fingers behind his head. He had already shed his jacket and rolled up his shirt-sleeves.

"I must tell you, Miss Carlton, I have only a few minutes to give you. But that's more than any other reporter is getting, so you should feel lucky. And of course you know my policy of not discussing the upcoming election." When Nancy and Bess nodded, he smiled. "Now, you wanted to talk to me about growing up in River Heights?"

"Yes, that's right," Nancy replied, flipping open her notebook and pretending to take notes.

The mayor launched into a long description of what the city was like when he was a boy. "Things have certainly changed for the better," he told them. "The old stereotypes are breaking down. We've even got our first female fire-fighter!"

"Doesn't it seem ironic, Mayor," Nancy said, smiling sweetly, "that you have such compassion for minorities and women, and yet you're being accused of sabotaging Caroline Hill's chance of becoming mayor?"

Filanowski glowered at Nancy. "If you're talking about the editorial in the *Morning Record*, that's a bunch of nonsense!" he said gruffly. "I am not trying to hurt Caroline Hill any more than I am trying to help Patrick Gleason."

"Then why have you remained silent?" Nancy persisted.

"I've already stated my reason!" Filanowski shouted, then hit the desk with his fist. "That's all I'll say on the matter! Why won't you people leave me alone!"

Nancy and Bess jumped in their seats. Why was he reacting so strongly to the questions? Nancy wondered.

"Excuse me," Filanowski mumbled, his face reddening. "I'm a little tense these days. It's not easy facing retirement. Now, where were we?"

At that moment, the mayor's intercom buzzed, and he hit the button. "Yes?"

"Al is on line one," Mrs. Wellborn said.

"Tell him I'll get back to him in five minutes," Filanowski replied. Then he stood up and turned to Bess. "Now, Miss Thomas," he said, "if you're ready to take my picture, we can wrap up this interview."

Nancy felt her heart sink. Obviously, the mayor had no intention of saying anything more about the election.

Bess chatted with the mayor about his retirement plans as she posed him next to a photograph of himself as a boy. Then she and Nancy thanked the mayor and left.

As they passed Mrs. Wellborn's desk, Nancy paused. "What will you do when Mayor Filanowski retires?" she asked pleasantly.

"I'm retiring to Florida also," Mrs. Wellborn answered. "Though I'm afraid I could never afford to live in Pelican Bay, where the mayor will be living. You have to be practically a millionaire to live there."

"Well, good luck," Bess told the secretary.

As soon as the girls had left City Hall, Bess said, "Filanowski really lost it when you asked him about Caroline. Do you think it means anything?"

"It makes me wonder if he has some special reason for not backing Caroline—something he doesn't want people to know," Nancy said. Then she shrugged. "But according to my dad, he's always been honest and straightforward. What could he possibly have to hide?"

They reached Nancy's Mustang, and Bess put Hector's camera bag in the backseat before she and Nancy climbed in front. "There's something else I don't get. How could the mayor afford an expensive condo in Florida?" Bess asked. "Didn't Hector tell us the mayor lost a lot of money a year ago?"

"That's right," Nancy said. "But I still don't see any connection between him and the frame-up. We'll just have to keep looking for clues. Come on, let's go to headquarters. I'm sure

Caroline and Hector will want to know how things went."

Fifteen minutes later, Nancy parked in front of Caroline's headquarters. They were just getting out of the car as Hector came to meet them, a concerned expression on his face.

"Don't worry, your camera's fine," Bess assured him, pointing to the bag on the backseat.

Nancy started to tell Hector about their interview, but he cut her off. "You can tell me all about the mayor later," he said tersely. "Right now you both have to go get Kyle."

"What are you talking about?" Bess asked, stopping on the sidewalk. "Where is he?"

"He was picked up by the police for trespassing and assault," he replied.

"What!" Nancy and Bess both exclaimed.

Hector held up a calming hand. "Apparently, he decided to stake out Patrick Gleason's house this morning, and something went wrong."

"Nan, let's get down there!" Bess said urgently.

"There's one other thing," Hector added.

Bess and Nancy turned to look at him.

"I don't mean to worry you," he cautioned, "but I think Kyle's been hurt."

Chapter

Eleven

HURT!" BESS CRIED. Her eyes widened in fear. "How badly? What happened?"

"All Kyle told me was that he'd been banged up in a fight," Hector replied.

Nancy and Bess didn't wait to hear anything more. They jumped back into Nancy's Mustang and drove to the police station. When they walked into the precinct room, Nancy spotted Kyle sitting on a chair near the desk sergeant.

Bess gasped as Kyle stood up and walked toward them. His shirt was torn, his left eye was swollen, and he had a gauze bandage on his forehead.

"Kyle, what happened to you! Are you all right?" Bess cried, running over to him.

Nancy stayed a few feet back as Kyle tipped

Bess's chin up so he could kiss her softly on the lips. "I got into a fight, sort of, with Steve Hill," Kyle explained, looking sheepishly from Bess to Nancy.

"Steve Hill?" Nancy repeated, confused. "But I thought you were at Patrick Gleason's house."

Kyle let out a long breath. "I'll explain everything, but let's just get out of here, okay? No one pressed charges, so I can go, but my car is still parked by Gleason's. Could you drop me off there?"

Bess got in the backseat with Kyle and made him lean his head back as he talked. "I'm not sure why I decided to stake out Gleason's house," he began, as Nancy pulled the car away from the curb. "I guess I just figured that it couldn't hurt, since we hadn't come up with any huge clues anywhere else.

"Anyway, I'd been standing across the street from the house for a while, and I hadn't seen anyone suspicious. I was just about to leave, when Steve Hill drove up."

"Did he see you?" Nancy asked, as she drove.

"Not at first," Kyle replied. "But when he came out five minutes later, instead of getting in his car, he crossed the street and walked toward me. He dropped a letter in the mailbox near me. I turned away, but he spotted me, anyway. I guess I'm a pretty crummy detective," he said apologetically.

95

Bess gently stroked his cheek. "That's not true. Staking out Gleason's house was a great idea, even if you didn't find out anything."

"What was Steve Hill doing at Gleason's house?" Nancy asked, looking at Kyle in the rearview mirror.

"I didn't exactly have a chance to find out," Kyle told her. "Hill grabbed me and asked what I was doing spying on Gleason. When I told him it was none of his business, he pushed me forward, away from him, and I stumbled and fell against the mailbox—that's how I bashed up my face. Pretty soon a squad car showed up. Mrs. Gleason had seen us fighting from her window, so she called the cops.

"Of course Steve Hill told the cops that I was spying on Gleason and that I'd attacked him," Kyle went on. "But I wasn't trespassing, and it was obvious that *I* was the only one hurt, so he didn't press charges. The police just brought me down to the station in a squad car to fill out a report."

Following Kyle's directions, Nancy made her way to Patrick Gleason's brick house and pulled up behind Kyle's yellow hatchback across the street. "I'm sorry you had to go through all that, Kyle."

"Especially since I didn't even find out anything," he said. "I guess I'd better go home, clean up, and get changed. What are you two up to?"

Nancy and Bess filled him in on their interview with Mayor Filanowski. "I have a feeling he may be hiding something, but I have no idea what," Nancy finished. "We haven't come up with anything incriminating on Patrick Gleason yet."

"And even though we know that Anna Dimitros knew Bobby Rouse, we don't have anything to prove that either she or Steve Hill is behind the frame-up," Bess put in. "We don't have any clues to what or who Greenwood is, either, or to who killed Bobby Rouse."

Nancy tapped the steering wheel thoughtfully. "We still haven't had a chance to talk to Ralph Lemko—he's the guy who posted bail for Bobby Rouse," she said. "Chief McGinnis gave me his address. What do you say we head over there, Bess?"

After saying goodbye to Kyle, the two girls drove to Lemko's. It turned out to be a small shingled house near the industrial part of River Heights.

"This isn't exactly a fancy neighborhood," Bess said. "I wonder how this Ralph Lemko guy got thirty thousand dollars to pay for Rouse's bail?"

"That's one of the things I hope we can find out by talking to him," Nancy said.

A slight, pale woman who introduced herself as Ralph's sister met Nancy and Bess at the door. "Ralph just left," the woman said.

"He was heading for Slim and Shorty's to have lunch."

The two friends thanked Ralph's sister and headed to the Mustang. "I guess it's back to Slim and Shorty's Good Eats Café," Bess said as they got into the car. "We're practically becoming regulars."

When they walked into the diner ten minutes later, Nancy immediately recognized the tall, wiry man she'd seen Bobby Rouse talking to the day he'd been killed. That had to be Ralph Lemko. He was sitting at a booth near the back, eating.

"Excuse me," Nancy asked as she and Bess slid into the booth. "Do you mind if my friend and I sit down?"

Ralph Lemko paused with his hamburger in midair and looked at Nancy as if she were a Martian. "You girls lost?" he asked gruffly. "The high school's back that way." He motioned with his head and stuffed the burger in his mouth.

"Thanks, but we're here to see you. You're Ralph Lemko, right?" Nancy asked. When he nodded, she added, "I'm trying to find out who killed your friend Bobby Rouse."

Lemko narrowed his eyes suspiciously and swallowed. "That's what we got cops for, you know."

"And detectives, like Nancy," Bess piped up. "We know that you posted Bobby Rouse's bail for him."

Lemko shot Bess a quick look of surprise.

"Thirty thousand dollars," Nancy added. "That's a lot of money."

The man lifted his glass to his mouth and eyed them over the rim. "So what?"

"Did someone give you that money?" Nancy asked. "If so, there's a chance that that person is the one who killed Rouse—he may have been afraid Bobby was going to talk about something." She eyed him sternly over the table. "In fact, the police might think you were working with the murderer and charge you as an accessory."

"I had nothing to do with Bobby's murder!" Lemko blurted out. "We were like brothers. He gave me the phone number of the person with the money himself!"

All right! Nancy thought. She was finally getting somewhere. "Was that Greenwood?" she asked, taking a shot in the dark.

"How'd you know about Greenwood?" Lemko asked, obviously taken aback. "From Bobby?"

Nancy shrugged nonchalantly. "Did you meet with Greenwood?"

"Of course not," Lemko replied, pushing a french fry around on his plate. "I never saw the guy."

"It was a guy?" Bess asked. "Did you talk to him over the phone?"

Lemko eyed Nancy and Bess skeptically. "I'm not saying any more. Why should I risk my neck by helping you? My friend is already dead."

"Did Bobby Rouse ever mention Steve Hill, or being interviewed by Anna Dimitros a few months ago?" Nancy asked, changing the subject.

Ralph Lemko broke into a grin for the first time. "Oh, her! What a ding-a-ling! I was with Bobby when she talked with him. All she asked him about were his *feelings* when he was on trial a few years ago. But that other guy, Hill, I never heard of him."

He shook his head. "You think that woman had something to do with Bobby getting killed?" he asked, pulling his wallet out of his back pocket. "I seriously doubt it. She was pretty ditzy."

With that, Ralph Lemko said goodbye, paid his bill, and left. Nancy and Bess looked at each other.

"I can't believe it," Bess said. "We finally talked to someone who knows Greenwood. Do you think Greenwood is the person who gave Lemko the bail money for Bobby Rouse?"

Nancy shrugged. "We still can't be sure, but he might be. I just wish we could track Greenwood down." She added, "The way Lemko talked, Anna Dimitros was so flaky it wouldn't be possible for her to be involved with the frame-up."

"That doesn't mean Anna's *not* involved,

though." Bess picked up the plastic menu in the booth and opened it. "Why don't we get some lunch?"

Nancy was hungry, too, and they ordered. Before long they were served burgers, fries, and soft drinks. "When I'm in love, I get hungry," Bess said, biting into her cheeseburger.

"So it *is* love?" Nancy asked, grinning at her friend. "You two are definitely cute together."

A slight blush colored Bess's cheeks. "Well . . . it's a little soon to really say *love,* but last night Kyle took me to the Mandarin Pagoda."

Nancy's eyebrows shot up. "That's the fanciest Chinese restaurant in town."

"Wasn't that nice of him? Nancy, he's the first guy I've met in a really long time who I feel totally relaxed with. But at the same time, I get all tingly every time I see him. Do you know what I mean?"

"Mm-hmm," Nancy said. "That's how I feel around Ned most of the time—when we're not fighting, that is." She told Bess about the real fight and the fake one she and Ned had had at Gleason's the day before.

Bess almost choked on her soda from laughing. "So have you crossed Gleason off your list of suspects?"

Nancy shrugged. "I think so, unless I happen to find something to connect him to the frame-up." She glanced at her watch. "Gosh, it's one-thirty. We'd better get back to Caroline's headquarters. I want to tell her about our interview with the mayor."

When Nancy and Bess walked into the campaign office, Caroline was rushing out of her office.

"Nancy, Bess!" Caroline cried, stopping short. "I'm glad you're here. I want to find out what Filanowski had to say, but I'm running late for my next speech."

"Well, he——" Nancy began.

"Caroline!" Hector called out from her office. "There's a phone call I think you should take."

"Can't it wait?" Caroline asked impatiently.

Looking through the office doorway, Nancy saw Hector hold out the receiver. "You'd better take it."

Caroline stepped back into her office. "Caroline Hill," she said brusquely into the receiver.

Her expression immediately softened, and she smiled. "Wayne, what a surprise!" As she listened, though, her smile faded, and her forehead creased. "I don't understand, Wayne," she said. "Why are you doing this to me? . . . I see." After a short pause, she hung up.

"That was my brother, Wayne Buckley," Caroline said in a shaky voice. She leaned against her desk, her face white.

"You have a brother?" Nancy asked, surprised. She had never heard Caroline mention him before.

Caroline nodded. "No one knows about him," she said. "Now he's trying to blackmail me!"

Chapter

Twelve

N ANCY AND BESS looked at each other in shock.

"Blackmail you? How? For what reason?" Hector asked. He looked as confused as Nancy felt.

"Wayne wants me to drop out of the race," Caroline said. "If I don't, he said he'll tell the papers that he and I have been running a fencing ring."

Bess laughed in disbelief. "But that's a lie. How could he prove it?"

"I've been sending him checks regularly for two years," Caroline explained. "Wayne just told me that he's been using the money to finance a fencing ring, and now he's going to tell everyone that I *knowingly* bankrolled the operation."

Nancy felt as if she'd just had the wind knocked out of her. "This is awful."

"Tell me about it," Caroline said.

"That's crazy," Hector scoffed.

Nancy wanted to agree, but a question nagged at her. "Why *were* you sending him money?"

Caroline looked around at the shocked faces staring at her. "I owe you all an explanation," she said, taking a deep breath. "I was adopted as an infant, when my parents died in a car crash. I always thought I was an only child, but a few years ago I found out that I had a brother eight years older than I."

"How did you find out about him?" Hector asked.

"Wayne saw a television news clip about one of my cases," Caroline said. "He was struck by my uncanny resemblance to our mother. He had always wondered what had happened to his baby sister, so he tracked me down."

"Why didn't he try to contact you before?" Nancy asked, fascinated by the story.

Caroline smiled wearily. "He said he figured he'd never be able to find me. I wonder now if he just didn't care. Anyway, he was pretty sure I was his sister because I still had the name Caroline that my natural parents had given me. So he called me up and said he wanted to get together. Of course, I was floored at the news that I had a brother. At first, I was skeptical, but I got hold of my adoption files and realized that he really *was* my brother."

"Wow," Bess breathed. "What a story!"

"Yes, or so it seemed," Caroline said. "I was thrilled. I pumped Wayne for everything he could remember about our parents. I think at first he was happy to see me, but then he decided that I made him feel bad."

"How's that?" Hector asked.

"He was ashamed of the way his life had turned out," Caroline replied. "He lives in a tenement in Chicago. He has two kids he adores, but his wife ran out on them five years ago, and he's been struggling just to keep food on the table. He's had about six jobs in the two years I've known him, and his car was just repossessed. He feels like a big screw-up, he said, and having a baby sister who's a successful lawyer just makes him feel worse. I told him that none of that mattered, but he said being around me made him feel worthless."

"So you left him alone, and that was that?" Nancy asked.

"No, that's the sticky part." Caroline sighed. "Wayne wasn't too proud to ask me to help out his kids financially. Of course I agreed. I saw how much Wayne's kids mean to him, and I felt guilty that he'd gotten a tough break as a kid. I grew up in a wonderful family, but Wayne was bounced around from one foster home to the next. Nobody really cared about him. So I agreed to send him a few hundred dollars every month to help out. That's where the checks come in."

Nancy was trying to make sense of all she was hearing. "But why would you leave a trail of checks if you're financing an illegal ring? Wouldn't you pay him in cash? And what about the money you would have gotten back from the fencing ring? Where's Wayne's proof of that?"

"I have no idea!" Caroline said, throwing up her hands. "Look, I know this must sound completely unbelievable to all of you. It does to me. But it just kills me that Wayne is doing this. What could he gain from my dropping out of the mayoral race?"

"Maybe he's jealous of your success," Bess suggested.

"You said he needs money," Nancy said gently. "Could someone be paying him to do this?"

"That's possible," Caroline replied, beginning to pace. "But who would that be? Nobody even knows I *have* a brother."

"Not even your husband, when you were married?" Nancy asked.

"No, we were splitting up then," Caroline said quietly. "I didn't want to tell anyone about Wayne until I was sure he really was my brother. Then he decided that he didn't want to get to know me. It hurt, you know. He's my only sibling."

"That's really sad," Bess murmured.

"Caroline, did Wayne give you any deadline

for dropping out of the mayoral race?" Nancy asked.

"Nine o'clock tomorrow morning."

"That doesn't give us a lot of time, but maybe it's enough to find out more about this fencing ring. I'd like to take a shot at talking to him, if that's okay with you."

"Sure." Caroline pulled an address book from her purse, then wrote down a number and address on a slip of paper and handed it to Nancy.

Hector pointed to his watch. "Caroline, we really have to get going to your next speaking engagement," he reminded her.

Caroline jumped. "My gosh, I forgot!" she exclaimed. "Nancy, let me know what you find out." Then she ran out of the office after Hector.

Nancy went over to Caroline's desk and used the phone to dial Wayne Buckley's number. She let the phone ring a long time before hanging up. "No one's there. I'll just have to try again later."

"Now what?" Bess asked.

Nancy drummed her fingers against the top of Caroline's desk. "So far, Anna Dimitros is the only suspect we've been able to connect to Bobby Rouse. I think we should visit her again."

"Maybe Wayne Buckley was one of those secrets about Caroline that Anna hinted at," Bess said. "Though I'm not sure how Anna could have found out about him." She frowned and added, "Do you think *Buckley* could be the person who sent that photograph and the story about the fencing ring to Steve Hill?"

"I don't know," Nancy said. She headed for the door, with Bess right behind her. "We certainly have a lot of questions. I just hope that this time we come up with some answers!"

Nancy and Bess parked in front of Anna Dimitros's building twenty minutes later, then made their way up the five flights to her apartment.

"Oh, it's you!" Anna frowned when she opened the door and saw Nancy and Bess. "Steve told me who you girls *really* are. You're spies for that Hill woman."

Looking past Anna, Nancy saw that Steve Hill was sitting on the living room couch. When he spotted Nancy, he jumped to his feet, sending a pile of papers flying to the floor.

"Call the police, Anna!" he snarled.

"Why bother?" Anna replied. "I'll just throw them out!" She started to slam the door shut, but Nancy managed to hold it open.

"Wait," Nancy said. "We'll be out of here in a flash, just as soon as you two tell me everything you know about Wayne Buckley, Caroline Hill's brother."

"What?" they said in unison, looking at Nancy as if she were crazy.

"That's right," Bess said. "He's trying to

109

blackmail Caroline into dropping out of the race."

Anna Dimitros looked so surprised that she didn't do anything to stop Nancy as she and Bess stepped past her into the living room.

"Wayne Buckley claims that he and Caroline ran a fencing ring together," Nancy explained.

"What does that have to do with Steve and me?" Anna demanded, sitting down on the couch beside him.

"You mentioned some big secrets you know about Caroline," Nancy said. "Could one of them be that she had a brother who was involved in a fencing ring?"

"No," Anna said. "The secrets that I know about her concern her own ruthless ambition."

"So you never knew about Caroline's brother?" Nancy asked, looking from Dimitros to Hill.

"I'm getting real sick of your questions," Hill said, his face turning red with anger.

Nancy faced him squarely and said, "If you gave me a straight answer, I wouldn't have to keep bugging you. If you're so convinced that the story about Caroline is true, why won't you tell us who gave you that information?"

Hill hesitated. "I don't know who sent me that stuff," he finally said. "The guy never gave me his name."

"But you talked to him, didn't you?" Bess asked.

"If it'll get you off my back, I might as well tell you," Steve Hill muttered. "I talked to him just once on the phone. He told me what he knew, and then he mailed some more information with the photo. The guy had a deep, resonant voice. That's all I know." He leaned over and gathered up the papers he'd spilled. "Now, why don't you two leave?"

Nancy and Bess exchanged a quick look. It was obvious that they weren't going to find out anything more. After saying goodbye, the two girls left.

"I don't believe we finally got Mr. Hill to tell us about the photo," Bess said as they hurried down the stairs.

"He practically admitted that he was fooled into going along with the fencing ring story. He doesn't even know who gave him the information!"

Bess gave her a sideways glance. "Unless he just said that to get you off his back."

"That's possible," Nancy agreed. "But they both seemed genuinely surprised to hear that Caroline had a brother. We can't be sure, but my gut feeling is that they were telling the truth."

When they got outside, Nancy paused next to her Mustang. "And I have another feeling that Wayne Buckley is the key to figuring out this whole case."

"I hope you can get in touch with him soon,"

Bess said. "But for now, I think I'd better get home. My aunt's in town, and my parents want me home before dinner."

Nancy dropped Bess off, then headed for home.

"Hi, Hannah!" Nancy called as she threw open the front door and went to the kitchen.

"You're home early from your volunteer work," Hannah said, and smiled. "Are you staying for dinner?"

Nancy grabbed an apple from a bowl of fruit on the kitchen table. "You bet," she replied, then headed for the stairs.

When she got to her room, Nancy glanced at the answering machine on her bedside table and saw it was blinking. She sat down on her bed and hit the message playback button.

"Nancy," a familiar voice said, "this is Mayor Filanowski calling."

"Uh-oh," Nancy muttered. "He found out I'm not the real Brenda Carlton."

The mayor's recorded voice sounded urgent. "I have something to tell you, Nancy. Meet me at the building site at the end of Summit Road, north of town, tomorrow morning at eight o'clock sharp. Don't tell anyone about this call or that you're meeting me tomorrow. Both our lives could be in serious danger if you do!"

Chapter

Thirteen

QUESTIONS RACED through her mind. What was so important? Why the cloak and dagger routine, with the deserted meeting place? Maybe she had been right about the mayor hiding something, Nancy thought. But did it have anything to do with Caroline? And why had the mayor decided to talk to *her* about it?

Adrenaline pumped through Nancy's body. She couldn't stand waiting until the next morning to talk to the mayor. Setting down her apple, she flipped through her address book to find the mayor's office number. When she dialed the number, Mrs. Wellborn answered the phone.

"I'm sorry, the mayor is gone for the day," the secretary replied in response to Nancy's question. "Would you like to leave a message?"

Nancy hesitated. "Er, no. But could you tell me where he can be reached?"

"I'm sorry, but I can't," Mrs. Wellborn replied. "You'll have to try again tomorrow."

Frustrated, Nancy hung up. Unfortunately, she didn't have the mayor's home number. She called information and was told the number was unlisted. Next, she called Caroline Hill's campaign office to see if she had the number, but Nancy was told the candidate was out campaigning and couldn't be reached.

Nancy lay down on her bed. "I can't just stay at home and do nothing!" she muttered, staring up at the ceiling. There were too many leads to follow—this secret business with the mayor, and finding out more about Wayne Buckley. . . .

Nancy sat up straight. Wayne Buckley! She could at least try to talk to him again. She picked up the receiver and dialed the number for Patrick Gleason's campaign office. If she was lucky, Ned would still be there.

She was put on hold, and then her boyfriend came on the line. "Ned! I'm glad you're there," Nancy told him. "How would you like to take a trip to Chicago with me this evening?"

"I don't know about that meeting tomorrow morning, Nan," Ned said several hours later, as he and Nancy drove toward Chicago. "You thought Filanowski was hiding something. He might want to meet you there so he can threaten you."

Nancy took her eyes briefly from the road to look at Ned. "If he was planning to hurt me, why would he leave that incriminating message on my machine?" she countered. "Besides, I don't have many leads in this case. I can't *not* go."

"Maybe you're right," Ned reluctantly agreed. "I just don't like the idea of your going alone. But at least you asked me to come with you to Wayne Buckley's. Someone who's willing to blackmail his own sister might be dangerous."

"He sounds pretty down and out," Nancy replied. "I'm still not sure Wayne is the one who called Steve Hill. Steve said that the guy he talked to had a deep, resonant voice, but that's about the only clue we have."

It was after seven o'clock before they found the street where Wayne Buckley lived. Ned had to squint in the fading sunlight to read the addresses. "This is it, Nan," he said, pointing to a doorway that was below sidewalk level.

"They live in a basement?" Nancy asked as she parked behind a rusty van.

Kids playing baseball in the street hit their ball Ned's way. He caught it and tossed it back. "Who knows," he said to Nancy in a low voice. "Two of those kids could be Buckley's."

Nancy nodded and went down the steps to Wayne Buckley's doorway. She heard a television on inside. When she rang the buzzer, she heard the sound switch off.

"Who is it?" a reedy voice demanded.

"My name is Nancy Drew. I'm here with my boyfriend, Ned," Nancy said loudly. "I want to talk to you about the phone call you made this afternoon to your sister, Caroline."

She had to wait a few moments before the door opened. The man standing there was in his early forties. His brown hair was thin and receding, and his creased face looked tired and defeated. His eyes skimmed over Nancy and Ned. Then he walked outside, went up a few steps, and looked up and down the street.

"Caroline didn't come?" he asked, eyeing them warily.

Nancy shook her head. Wayne seemed to think this over for a second. "I guess that's okay," he decided. He came back down the steps and led them into his living room. Then he turned around. "So is she taking me up on my offer?"

Nancy and Ned stood just inside the door. In the center of the room was a huge television set and a well-worn easy chair with a racing car magazine splayed across the arm. The floor was scattered with toys, schoolbooks, and homework papers.

Nancy decided to call his bluff. "No, Wayne, she's not dropping out of the race. I'm here to find out why you're blackmailing your sister. I doubt there even *is* a fencing ring. Or if there is, there's no way Caroline is involved."

"Why are you doing this?" Ned asked, picking up on Nancy's reasoning. "Is someone paying you?"

Wayne grabbed an open can of soda sitting on the television set and took a big gulp. "She told you that I was lying? I figured she would," he said. "Well, it's not a lie. And nobody is paying me anything. I'm blowing the whistle on her because I don't think it's right that she should be mayor when she's committed a crime." Wayne took another swallow of soda and gave them a self-righteous look.

Ned snorted with disbelief. "Are you the one who leaked the fencing ring story that ended up in *Today's Times?*"

"Yeah. So?" Wayne asked.

Nancy stared at him. Steve Hill had said the person he spoke to had a deep voice, but Wayne Buckley's voice was pretty high. What was his game, anyway? "Then why did you give Steve Hill a doctored photograph?" she asked. "Why didn't you just send the canceled checks as proof in the first place?"

"My mistake," Wayne replied. "I didn't think I had enough proof, so I staged that photograph with Rouse. It was a reenactment of what actually happened, only it wasn't Caroline in the photograph. But it could've been!"

Nancy and Ned exchanged a look. "Did you know that the man in that photograph, Bobby Rouse, was murdered?" Nancy asked.

Wayne shifted his eyes nervously. "So what? He was a hood, and he got into trouble."

"What about Greenwood?" Nancy asked. "Is he the one who convinced you to blackmail your sister?" She knew it was a shot in the dark, but she had to try everything.

Wayne crushed his soda can and pointed it at them. "I don't know what you're talking about," he said. "Look, I have proof of the fencing operation. And I'm talking about more than the canceled checks. I'll show you."

Waving for Nancy and Ned to follow, he stalked down a hallway to a doorway and flicked on the overhead light. Surrounding a narrow bed were stacks of stereo equipment boxes. Nancy looked more closely. There had to be at least a hundred CD players stashed there.

"Yikes!" Ned whistled, running his hand over a pile of boxes. "This bundle must be worth thousands! Where did you get all these from?"

Wayne laughed and grabbed a box. "Let's just say they fell off a truck." He fished his key chain out of his pants pocket, then slit the factory tape open with a key. "And this is just one day's shipment," he said proudly. "Caroline puts up the money that this load cost, then I turn around and sell it again for two, maybe three times that. She gets half the profit, and I get half."

118

Nancy felt her stomach sink. All Wayne had to do was call *Today's Times* with this story, and Caroline's chances of winning would be zilch.

"How can you prove that Caroline received any money from you?" Nancy asked Wayne.

"I can't, she got paid in cash," Wayne explained. He pulled a shiny black CD player out of its protective foam shell. "It's a nice little operation," he said, holding the player up for Ned and Nancy to inspect. "But I can't be doing this stuff anymore. I've got an obligation to my kids to go straight." For the first time, Nancy saw his expression soften.

"This is pretty impressive, Wayne," Ned said lightly, looking around the room. "But do you realize how much you're hurting your sister by pretending that she's financing this operation?"

"I'm not pretending," Wayne insisted. He shepherded Nancy and Ned out of the room ahead of him.

Suddenly the front door banged open, and a boy who looked about eight years old zipped past Nancy and Ned. "Dad," he pleaded, hopping on one foot in front of Wayne while he juggled a baseball in his hands. "Can Suzy and I have some money for the ice cream truck? Please please please?"

Wayne's expression softened again. He reached into his pocket, then handed the boy a few dollars. "Here," he said. "Now, make sure you share this with your sister."

"Thanks!" Tommy exclaimed. As he took the money, he accidentally dropped his ball, and it rolled into the bedroom. Tommy ran after it and dove behind a stack of CD boxes. With a look of panic, Wayne ran in after him.

"Tommy, be careful in here!" he shouted, just as Tommy knocked into the boxes with one knee, causing the whole stack to rock. With a light touch, Wayne quickly steadied the boxes.

As Nancy watched from the doorway, a warning bell went off in her head. Wait a minute, she thought. Something about those boxes isn't right. Heavy audio components shouldn't be so easy to move.

She pulled Ned aside in the living room, while Wayne shooed his son out the door. "Try to distract Wayne in the kitchen," Nancy whispered to Ned. "I want to take another look at those boxes."

As Caroline's brother rejoined her and Ned, Nancy said, "Wayne, I'd like to get a photo of these CD players to show Caroline."

"Sure, why not?" Wayne shrugged.

"My camera's in the car," Nancy fibbed. "I'll be right back."

As Nancy slipped out the front door, she heard Ned ask Wayne for a drink of water. She paused outside the door for a moment, holding it open a crack until she heard the two men walk into the kitchen at the far end of the apartment. Ned was telling Wayne that he believed him, not Caroline, and Wayne fell for it.

Good work, Nickerson! Nancy thought.

Walking on tiptoe, Nancy sneaked back into the bedroom and lifted one of the boxes. It couldn't have weighed more than a few ounces— much lighter than it would be if it contained a CD player.

The box had to be empty! No wonder Wayne had managed to steady the stack so easily.

Reaching down, Nancy picked up the whole stack of seven CD boxes. They *all* felt empty.

Her excitement built as she quickly checked the other stacks. Except for the one Wayne Buckley had opened for her and Ned, every single one was so light that Nancy knew they were empty.

Her suspicions had been right. Wayne had filled this room with boxes so that it *looked* as if there was a fencing ring. But his stolen electronics story was really a big fake.

Chapter
Fourteen

Nancy's heart leapt. Finally she had some solid proof that would help prove Caroline's innocence.

Trying to control her excitement, Nancy sneaked back to the front door. She pretended to be coming in from her car and shut the door loudly behind her. Then she walked into the kitchen, where Wayne Buckley and Ned were still talking.

"I must have left my camera at home," she said, trying to look disappointed. She decided not to confront Wayne about the empty boxes. She was fairly certain he wasn't in this operation alone, and confronting him would give him enough time to stock up on *real* CD players before leaking his story to the press. Then Nancy would have a much harder time proving that the whole thing was a scam.

Turning to Wayne, Nancy asked, "Why didn't you go directly to the newspaper with the fencing ring story in the beginning? Why did you pick Caroline's ex-husband to talk to?"

"Who?" Wayne asked.

"Steve Hill, Caroline's ex," Ned explained, shooting Nancy a glance. Wayne didn't seem to know who Steve Hill was!

"Oh, right!" Wayne said in a rush. "Steve Hill." He laughed nervously. "I knew he wasn't crazy about Caroline, so I called him. I was hoping I could avoid getting myself in trouble, but that didn't work out."

"I see," Nancy said blandly. She was beginning to think that someone else, not Wayne, had given Steve Hill the story about Caroline. Now that person was using Wayne to back up the story.

Wayne clapped Ned on the shoulder and escorted Nancy and Ned out onto the sidewalk. "Then I'll be hearing from Caroline tomorrow?" he asked. "I mean, she won't still run for mayor once she hears that you've seen the evidence, right?"

"She'll call you at nine A.M.," Nancy assured him. After saying goodbye, she and Ned walked to her car.

As they drove away, Nancy told Ned about the empty boxes.

"Wow! You're kidding! Well, that takes the sting out of Wayne's threat to Caroline," Ned remarked. He pulled a map of Chicago from the doorflap and consulted it for the best way back to the highway. "What will you do now? Will Caroline confront him?"

"I guess that's up to her," Nancy replied, stopping at a red light. "The thing is, someone else besides Wayne *has* to be involved in this fencing scheme. If Wayne was involved in a real fencing operation, he'd have to implicate himself as well as Caroline, which he wouldn't do. Besides, Steve Hill told Bess and me that the person who gave him the story had a deep, resonant voice."

"Which Wayne Buckley definitely doesn't have," Ned put in. "Also, it was pretty obvious that Wayne was lying when he said he called Steve. Wayne couldn't even remember who the guy was." He pointed ahead. "Make a right here. The highway entrance is just ahead."

Nancy nodded, turning her car to the right. "That leaves the question of who it was that Steve Hill *did* talk to. Could it have been Greenwood?"

"Whoever that is," Ned added.

"Mmm. I hope to have another lead tomorrow morning after I talk to the mayor," Nancy said. "My meeting's at eight, so maybe I can get back to Caroline with any new leads before she has to give Wayne an answer."

Nancy certainly hoped so. Caroline's whole future could depend on it.

Nancy woke up the next morning at six-thirty, feeling nervous. A cold, drizzling rain didn't ease her mood at all as she got in her Mustang to go meet the mayor.

With her radio blasting rock music, Nancy drove north through town and turned onto Summit Drive, a narrow road that wound up into the hills overlooking the town. Nancy passed nothing but trees. She drove a mile or so through the rain-soaked woods to the top of the hill, where Summit Drive ended abruptly in muddy tire tracks that led into a small clearing.

Nancy peered through her rain-blurred windshield: no sign of another car. She got out of her Mustang and pulled up the hood of her yellow rain slicker, then trudged through the mud into the clearing. She saw nothing but tree stumps, a huge boulder jutting ten feet or so out of the ground, and a sign nailed to a tree off to one side of the tire tracks.

Looking around uneasily, Nancy walked over to read the sign. It was a legal notice stating that a hearing was scheduled for the end of the next week to rezone the land for an incinerator.

That's odd, Nancy thought. She hadn't heard anything about an incinerator being built. Wouldn't Caroline have known about it? With her strong environmental stance, Caroline would definitely have an opinion about the effects an incinerator would have on the town's air quality.

She read on to the end of the notice, then gasped when she saw the name of the company that had requested the hearing.

"Greenwood Incorporated!" Nancy said aloud. So Greenwood wasn't the name of a person at all: It was the name of a *corporation*.

How did Greenwood Incorporated fit into the frame-up of Caroline and Bobby Rouse's murder? Nancy wondered. Whoever ran Greenwood would have every reason to want to make sure that Caroline *wasn't* elected mayor. With her record, Caroline was sure to fight any plan that would pollute the environment as much as an incinerator would.

And that meant that whoever ran Greenwood Inc. had every reason to want Caroline to *lose* the election. This put a whole new angle on the case!

Nancy's thoughts were interrupted as a black sedan pulled up behind her car. Mayor Filanowski climbed out of the car and made his way over to her.

"Good, you're here," he said simply. "I was afraid you wouldn't show up." He was wearing a black raincoat, a hat, and boots.

"Of course I came," Nancy said, turning her face up in the rain to look at him. "And my guess is that you didn't call me up here to yell at me for fooling you. Am I right?"

"Oh, that." Filanowski chuckled. "I think

Miss Carlton was the one who was most upset. We both found out we'd been fooled when she called me to confirm her appointment on Friday. Somehow, she figured out that it was you." The mayor started walking into the clearing. "That's when I realized that you were that young detective I've heard so much about."

Nancy walked alongside the mayor. "Why did you want to talk to me?"

Filanowski smiled. "I'll get to that in a second," he told her. "Let's climb up on this rock. You can get a good view of the city from here."

Trying to keep her curiosity in check, Nancy started up the rock. The climb wasn't steep, but the rock was slick under Nancy's grip as she scrabbled up. "Are you sure you should be doing all this with your heart condition?" Nancy asked, giving Filanowski a hand up.

"No, I'm not," he grunted, "so don't tell my doctor." At the top he stood and looked around. All around them were trees. At the foot of the hill, Nancy could make out the gray outline of River Heights through the rain.

"Nancy," the mayor began, gazing out, "I had to wait until this morning to tell you because I wanted to make one more attempt to convince an old friend that what he was doing was wrong. Unfortunately, he wouldn't listen to me."

Convince who? Nancy wanted to shout. And what's he doing? But she had a feeling the mayor wouldn't be hurried, so she kept quiet.

"He's been my friend since he moved here ten years ago," Filanowski went on. "He's done very well in business, and he's made many generous contributions to the town, including a new hospital wing. Then, six months ago, he came to me with an idea: He wanted to build an incinerator on this site, to burn the town's garbage. However, he didn't want to follow the city's restrictions on the amount that he could burn."

"That's not fair—" Nancy started to say, but the mayor held up a hand to silence her.

"My friend convinced me to loosen the regulations and allow him to sell his incinerator service to other cities as well as River Heights. Chicago, for instance, is desperate to get rid of its excess garbage. That way, he could make a much bigger profit. In return, he planned to donate money to build a new public library for the city."

"But in the meantime, his incinerator would be belching out pollution," Nancy argued.

Filanowski nodded, a guilty look in his eyes. "At the time, it seemed like a small price to pay for a badly needed library that the city's budget just couldn't afford. I can see now that I was wrong. I guess I had become arrogant. I thought that after fifteen years in office, I knew better than anyone what was best for River Heights.

"Anyway," he continued, "as mayor, I have control over who gets awarded contracts. My friend's plan made sense, so I agreed to go along with it and look the other way when his incinerator took in too much garbage."

Nancy's eyes widened with shock. The mayor had just admitted to breaking the law! "But why would you . . ." Before she even finished asking her question, she knew the answer. "He paid you off, didn't he?" she guessed. "That's how you can afford to retire to that expensive place in Florida."

Filanowski looked surprised. "You *are* a good detective, aren't you? I didn't take any money at first. That came later, after my heart attack, when my doctor told me I couldn't stay on as mayor much longer. When my friend realized that the next mayor might be Caroline Hill, a strong environmentalist, he bought me that condo and convinced me to turn my back on Caroline and withhold my endorsement of her."

He let out a weary sigh. "He convinced me that it would be in the best interests of River Heights in the long run. I convinced myself that the money was just a generous gift from an old friend, but now I see it for the bribe that it was. I was desperate," the mayor said. "I had lost all my money a year ago, and I was being forced to retire. I swear to you, I had no idea that my friend would take it so far."

"You mean when he made up the fencing ring story, don't you?" Nancy asked.

The mayor nodded. "When I saw that article

on Monday, I knew it was a lie. I asked my friend if he knew anything about it, and he admitted that he'd thought the story up," he explained. "I told him he was crazy. Then, when I read in the paper that Bobby Rouse had been murdered, I realized that he truly *is* insane."

Nancy could barely contain her excitement. The mayor was telling her that the same person was responsible for setting up Caroline *and* for killing Bobby Rouse! "Who is it?" she asked urgently. "You have to tell me!"

Mayor Filanowski hesitated, then said, "I could have just given you his name right away, but I wanted you to hear—"

Suddenly the mayor took a sharp breath, and his eyes bulged out. As Nancy watched in horror, his knees buckled and he toppled backward. He fell face up at the base of the rock.

When Nancy saw the dark red stain spreading across his left shoulder, she realized what had happened.

Sam Filanowski had been shot!

Chapter

Fifteen

FOR A MOMENT, all Nancy could do was stare at Mayor Filanowski lying at the base of the rock. She was about to bend down, to see if she could find a pulse, when she heard a zing as a piece of rock chipped off next to her feet. Now someone was shooting at *her!*

Nancy glanced around wildly. Another bullet whistled over her head, and she leapt off the rock, landing on her hands and knees in the mud, next to the mayor. At least now the big rock was between the shooter and her and the mayor.

She felt a rush of relief when she heard him groan. "Thank goodness you're alive! Hang in there," Nancy said.

The mayor tried to sit up, but Nancy gently rested him back against the rock. She yanked a handkerchief out of his pocket and pressed it to the wound on his shoulder. Within a few seconds the handkerchief was saturated with blood.

Mayor Filanowski groaned again, and his eyes flickered. Nancy's eyes searched frantically around her, and she tried to ignore the panic that was building inside her. How was she ever going to get them out of there?

Suddenly Nancy heard a car roar up to where she'd parked. There was the squeal of brakes and then the sound of a car door opening and slamming shut. She tried to stifle her fear. Did the shooter have an accomplice?

"Nancy Drew!" a familiar voice rang out a moment later. "Where are you? I know all about your lies!"

"Brenda!" Nancy breathed in disbelief. "What are you doing here! Stay down!" she cried out.

Keeping low, Nancy edged along the rock and peeked around it. Brenda was standing on the edge of the road next to Nancy's car, holding an umbrella.

"Brenda, get back in your car!" Nancy shouted. "Someone is shooting at us."

Brenda didn't seem to have heard her. "Where are you?" Brenda demanded, looking around. "You're in big trouble, Nancy. You'd better come out!"

Just then another shot ricocheted off the rock a few inches from Nancy, and Nancy ducked. This time, she could tell where the shot had come from: the trees just to the right of the cars and about fifteen feet to Brenda's left.

Nancy sneaked a second quick peek and saw Brenda gingerly putting one high-heeled foot forward into the muddy tire tracks. The shooter was using a silencer, so Brenda had no idea that she was in danger. In a second she was going to walk right into the line of fire!

"Big trouble is right," Nancy muttered. "Brenda," she shouted again, "stay back, or you'll get shot!"

"What?" Brenda called, taking another step into the mud. Nancy glanced over her shoulder at Filanowski propped against the rock and groaning slightly. What a mess! The mayor was wounded, and Brenda could get shot any second. Nancy knew she couldn't just stay behind the rock forever. She had to do something.

She took a deep, steadying breath. "Here goes," she muttered. Shedding her rain slicker so it wouldn't get in her way, she darted out into the clearing, running in a jagged line with her head and shoulders tucked down. It seemed to take her hours to cross the thirty feet to Brenda, who was looking at Nancy as if she had gone crazy. Nancy grabbed Brenda's arm and yanked her around.

"Hey! What—" Brenda's objection was cut short as a bullet pierced her umbrella, knocking it out of her hand.

"Come on, Brenda, or you'll get killed," Nancy said through clenched teeth. She pulled Brenda ten feet back, to the safety of her Mustang. Nancy threw open the passenger door, pushed Brenda in, then ran around the back of the car and jumped in the driver's side.

"Wa-was that a gunshot?" Brenda stammered, hunching low in the seat.

"Yes, it was," Nancy said, revving the engine of her Mustang. "Keep your head down."

Her tires splattered muddy water as she threw the car into gear and plowed across the clearing to the other side of the rock. Brenda gasped when she saw Filanowski lying there.

"Oh, my gosh, he's bleeding!"

Nancy had already jumped out of the car. "Quick, Brenda, give me a hand," she called. "We have to get him to a hospital right away!"

Filanowski was barely conscious and was shivering from shock as they tugged and pulled him to the Mustang. Nancy didn't know how they managed it, but somehow she and Brenda got the mayor into the backseat. No sooner was he inside than he lost consciousness. *Please* let him be all right, Nancy silently begged.

Two more gunshots whistled over their heads as Nancy unlocked the trunk of her car and thrust a blanket at Brenda. "Here, get in the car and cover him up with this," she said urgently. "We have to get out of here before we all get killed!"

For once, Brenda was speechless. She quickly did as Nancy asked. Seconds later, they were all back in the car, and Nancy sped out of the clearing.

"Nancy, who was shooting at us?" Brenda asked. Her hazel eyes were wide with fear, and her face was white.

"I'm not sure," Nancy replied. It seemed clear to her, though, that the "friend" the mayor had told her about wasn't such a good friend after all. She shuddered at the thought. She was dealing with a crazed, evil man. Nancy gazed worriedly at the mayor in the rearview mirror. Until he regained consciousness, she couldn't find out who the person was.

It seemed an eternity before Nancy pulled up at the emergency entrance of the River Heights General Hospital. A team of medics rushed the mayor inside.

Nancy knew she would have to answer the staff's questions, but first she needed to make a phone call. She hurried to a pay phone in the emergency room, then called Kyle at her father's law office.

"Hi, Nan, what's up?" Kyle asked cheerfully.

"Kyle, I need you to drop everything you're doing," Nancy told him. "Tap into the state's computer records on businesses incorporated in River Heights in the last year. Look for Greenwood Incorporated, and find the name of the person who filed the incorporation forms. Can you do that?"

"So that's what Greenwood means!" Kyle exclaimed. "No problem, Nan. I should be able to find that out right away."

"Great," Nancy replied. "Then, see if you can find Bess and meet me here at R. H. General. Someone just shot Sam Filanowski, and I don't want to leave until I'm sure he's going to be all right."

Next, Nancy called Caroline Hill at her campaign headquarters. By now it was a little after nine, and Caroline was there waiting for Nancy. After telling Caroline what had happened, Nancy asked her to hold off on giving her brother an answer about dropping out of the election. "If we can just wait until the mayor tells us who's behind the fencing story, then we can confront Wayne with facts he won't be able to deny."

Nancy was just hanging up when Brenda tapped her on the shoulder. "Nancy, I've told the people in the emergency room all I know. Now I'm going to catch a cab home," Brenda said. She wrinkled her nose in distaste. "Hospitals give me the creeps!"

After Brenda left, Nancy was tied up for a half-hour explaining the details of the shooting, first to the emergency room's attending physician and then to the police. She finally managed to break away and flag down a nurse, who told her that the mayor was being moved up to the Intensive Care Unit. Luckily, the bullet had only grazed his shoulder, and he would not require surgery.

"Where is Intensive Care?" Nancy asked.

"On the third floor." The nurse pointed with her clipboard. "It's in the Blount wing."

Nancy stared blankly at the woman. "The Blount wing?" she echoed. "You mean the *Alan* Blount wing?"

The nurse nodded impatiently. "Just take the elevator and follow the signs."

That's it! Nancy realized. The mayor had told her that his "friend" had donated a wing to the hospital. It *had* to be Alan Blount! And that meant that Blount was behind the scheme to get Caroline to back down from the mayoral campaign. Nancy was willing to bet that when Kyle told her the name of the person who was in charge of Greenwood, it would be none other than Alan Blount. She still wasn't sure why Blount had backed *Caroline's* campaign, but she didn't have time to worry about that right now.

Nancy picked up her pace as she headed for the elevator. If she could just talk to the mayor right away and get him to admit that it was Blount, then they could call the police to arrest the man before he hurt someone else. There wasn't a moment to lose!

As she stepped into the elevator car, she heard Bess's voice call out, "Nancy, wait!" A second later Bess and Kyle threw themselves into the elevator with her.

"We found out who Greenwood is!" Kyle gasped.

"Alan Blount, right?" Nancy said.

Bess blinked in surprise. "How did you know?"

"I'll tell you later," Nancy said. "I've got to talk to the mayor, but they won't let us all go into Intensive Care. Follow my lead, okay?"

Bess and Kyle nodded. When the elevator doors opened at the third floor, Nancy hurried over to the nurses' station. "I've got to see my father, Sam Filanowski," she said urgently. "Where is he?"

Glancing behind Nancy at Bess and Kyle, the nurse said, "Your friends will have to wait here." Then she led Nancy through a set of swinging doors, down a hallway, and into a room with a hospital bed and all kinds of monitors. The mayor was still unconscious and was connected to an intravenous unit and some monitors. A doctor in a surgeon's mask and green uniform stood at the foot of the bed, looking at a chart.

"Oh, Doctor," the nurse said, "I didn't realize you were in here."

The doctor turned around briefly and gave them a short nod.

"I'm afraid you can only have fifteen minutes with your father," the nurse told Nancy. Then she left, closing the door behind her.

Nancy nodded and turned to the doctor. "I'm glad you're here," Nancy said. "I was afraid he would be all alone."

"Really?"

Something about the doctor's deep, gravelly voice made Nancy take a closer look at him. He seemed familiar somehow. . . . Taking in the man's graying blond hair and pale gray eyes, she realized that she *did* know him.

"Alan Blount!" Nancy exclaimed.

For a split second his eyes widened in surprise. Then, in a swift move, Blount jumped forward and grabbed Nancy by the shoulders, wrapping his arm around her neck in a choke hold. Before she could move, he pressed her against the wall and pinned her arms behind her back. With his free hand, he reached for something on the bedside table. Nancy's eyes widened in terror as she saw what he had picked up.

"I think there's enough serum in here to finish off both you and the mayor," Blount rasped, holding a hypodermic needle up to her face.

"I'm not the only one who knows what you've done!" Nancy blurted out. "There's no point in killing me. My friends will still tell the police."

Alan Blount tightened his hold on her arms. "That may be. But with you out of the way, I can at least buy enough time to get out of the country." In a disgusted tone, he added, "My plans are ruined now, anyway, so there's no reason to stay. I should have done everything myself, instead of counting on spineless men like Filanowski and Rouse."

"Is that why you killed Bobby?" Nancy asked, her heart racing. "Because you thought he would rat on you after he got arrested?" Nancy turned her head to see Blount's face behind her.

Blount grunted in assent. "What a mistake I made, trusting that idiot. It was easy enough giving Rouse's friend Ralph the money to post bail. The guy was happy to get his friend out, so he never questioned who Mr. Greenwood was or why I would fork over thirty thousand dollars to free Bobby. Once Rouse was out of jail, I made sure he'd never spill the beans on me—ever."

Nancy shivered at Blount's cold tone. Somehow she had to buy some time before he decided to use that syringe! "Your fencing ring frame-up was pretty clever," she said. "You're the one who had Bobby Rouse pose in that fake photograph. And then you fed the story to Steve Hill."

Blount let out a short laugh. "It *was* clever of me, wasn't it?" he said. "Steve Hill was so ready to believe the story that he didn't even ask any questions. Too bad you had to stick your nose into things and prove the photograph was a fake. I'd covered my tracks so well up to that point— I'd even given money to Caroline Hill's campaign."

That explained why Nancy had seen him encouraging Patrick Gleason before the debate. He wasn't really for Caroline Hill at all! "I can see why you wouldn't want Caroline to be mayor," Nancy said. "She'd never go along with your incinerator plan. But what makes you think that Patrick Gleason would?"

"He'd be a perfect mayor," Blount said. "He doesn't have much experience, and he's eager to please."

Nancy was too disgusted to comment. There was still one piece to this puzzle that she hadn't fit into place yet. "What about Wayne Buckley? When did you get *him* involved in the scam?"

"I had to work hard to find out about Buckley. After the paper printed their retraction, I was desperate to ruin Caroline Hill's campaign. Through my professional contacts, I got hold of Caroline's bank statements and scoured them for any scandal I could smear her with. That's how I found out about her payments to Wayne Buckley. A little more checking, and I traced him to Chicago. When I visited Buckley, he told me all about the money she sent him for his kids every month."

"And you somehow convinced him to pretend that she was sending the money to finance a fencing ring, right?" Nancy guessed. "How did you scare Buckley into blackmailing his sister?"

"His children, of course! I had that poor jerk convinced that I could report him to the authorities as an unfit father and have them taken away for good." Alan Blount gave a harsh laugh. "It was a great ploy. Only you came along and messed everything up! I couldn't believe it when Filanowski told me that you had been asking questions. I could tell he was turning chicken. It's a good thing I decided to follow him this morning, or he would have told you everything."

"But you—"

"That's enough!" Blount snapped. He pulled Nancy's head back.

Nancy felt a drop of sweat roll down her forehead. Out of the corner of her eye, she could see Blount bringing the needle closer to her neck. She felt it prick her flesh.

She was about to be injected with poison!

Chapter

Sixteen

NANCY SWALLOWED HARD. She tried to move, but Blount held her against the hospital room wall.

"Don't do it!" Nancy said hoarsely. "The nurse will be back any second."

"There's plenty of time," Blount whispered.

Just then a faint groan broke the silence of the room. Startled, Blount glanced over at Filanowski and moved the needle a few inches away from Nancy's neck.

That split second was all Nancy needed. Wrenching her body backward, she pushed Blount off balance. He tried to force her against the wall again, but she managed to free an arm and jab him in the ribs with her elbow.

"Kyle! Bess!" Nancy shouted at the top of her lungs. "Help! Quick!"

Blount whirled at her again, the syringe poised, but Nancy lashed out with a judo kick, and the needle flew from his grasp. Seconds later Kyle and Bess burst into the room. Kyle rushed at Blount and slugged him in the jaw. Blount staggered backward a few feet, and Kyle and Nancy were able to pin his hands behind his back.

"I'll call the police!" Bess cried, running from the room.

Nancy was still trying to catch her breath when she heard the mayor groan again. Looking up, she saw him open his eyes and look groggily around.

"What . . . ?" he began when he saw Nancy, Kyle, and Alan Blount.

Nancy smiled at him. "You can relax, Mayor Filanowski. Everything's under control."

"I propose a toast to the new mayor of River Heights, Caroline Hill!" Kyle proclaimed, raising his glass of ginger ale.

A week had passed since Alan Blount's arrest. A few days earlier, Caroline had been elected in a landslide. To celebrate, she had invited Nancy, Carson Drew, Hector, Kyle, Kyle's sister Mary, Bess, and Ned to an Italian restaurant.

"To Caroline!" everyone at the table cried, clinking glasses.

"I'm not officially mayor yet," Caroline reminded them with a laugh. "The inauguration is still two weeks away."

"But the hard part is over," Hector said, spearing a cherry tomato with his fork. "After all you've been through, you deserve to celebrate."

"It was a rough week on all of us," Caroline agreed. She took a piece of Italian bread and began buttering it. Glancing over at Ned, she said, "I'm especially glad that you came tonight, Ned. I know you believed in Patrick Gleason as a candidate. I respect that you stood by him, yet you didn't let your loyalty stand in the way when Nancy had to investigate him. That takes a lot of strength."

Nancy looked fondly at Ned. She was grateful to Caroline for acknowledging Ned's sticky role in her investigation.

"I did want Gleason to win," Ned remarked. "But that doesn't mean I don't think you'll be a good mayor. From what everyone tells me, you'll be terrific."

Caroline smiled. "Thank you, Ned."

"What's going to happen to your brother, Caroline?" Carson Drew asked.

Caroline smiled ruefully. "I decided not to press charges for blackmailing—I just couldn't do that to my own brother. But it's going to take a long time for me to trust him again."

"Still, he did go on the evening news to tell people that you were an innocent victim of Alan Blount's scheming," Bess put in. "That must count for something."

Caroline nodded. "It does. Wayne promised

that he would volunteer in some community organizations, too, to try to make up for what he did. He also said he finally realized that he needs to take more responsibility to make life better for himself and his children. If he really means that, then we'll be able to become a lot closer."

"And hopefully he'll never let people like Alan Blount take advantage of him again," Bess added.

Caroline took a sip of water, then said, "Alan Blount won't be able to bother anyone for a good long time. I heard from the new D.A. that they're going to ask for twenty years when they prosecute him. And Mayor Filanowski told me that when he testifies in Blount's trial, he's going to tell the jury everything, regardless of how it reflects on him."

"Good for him," Ned said fiercely. "It's the least he could do."

Nancy let out a sigh. "I know what the mayor did was wrong, but I can't help feeling sorry for him," she said. "It took a lot of guts to go public, and he might end up in jail."

"I'm just glad that he decided to make a public announcement about his involvement with Alan Blount before the election," Nancy's father added. "And he's going to sell the condominium that Blount bought him and donate the money to the city. Maybe the court will realize that he's trying to make amends and go easy on him."

"What about Anna Dimitros and Steve Hill?" Bess asked, wiping her mouth with her napkin.

"They must be disappointed that you *weren't* involved in that fake fencing ring," Kyle chimed in.

Caroline burst into laughter. Seeing everyone stare at her, she explained, "It just so happens that Anna Dimitros called me this afternoon and said that she wants to work with me."

"What?" Nancy and Bess chorused.

Caroline nodded. "She said that when she and Steve saw the mayor and Wayne on the evening news, they realized they'd been all wrong about me. Originally, she was planning to write a 'tell-all' book about me, but when she realized I'm not the power-hungry person she thought, Anna decided to scrap the book."

"All she told us," Nancy said, "was that it was a nonfiction book. I assumed it had something to do with her trial and imprisonment. So what's she going to do now?"

Caroline smiled. "Anna has a new project. She wants to help me write my autobiography. Can you believe it?" She shook her head and laughed. "Pretty nervy, eh?"

"Speaking of nervy," Nancy said, "I found out from Brenda how she knew about my meeting with Mayor Filanowski last week."

"This should be good," Ned muttered.

Nancy smiled at him. "After Brenda found out

that I had, in her words, 'stolen the greatest interview of her life,' she was ready to kill me. So she marched over to my house, but I had just left for Chicago with Ned. She gave Hannah some excuse about leaving something for me in my bedroom. I had saved the mayor's message on my machine, and she, being nosy, wanted to see if there was anything on my machine. She heard the mayor's message about meeting him on Summit Drive."

"Unbelievable," Hector said, shaking his head.

"Ahem!" Kyle cleared his throat. "I'd like to propose another toast," he declared.

Bess giggled. "Another one?"

"Yes," Kyle replied. "This time, I'd like to make a toast to Nancy and Carson Drew."

Nancy and her father looked at each other in surprise.

"To Mr. Drew," Kyle said, smiling at Nancy's father, "for hiring me at his law firm one week and then letting me take half the next week off."

"And then making you work overtime the next week!" Carson added with a laugh.

"True," Kyle agreed. "But if you hadn't let me work on Caroline Hill's campaign, I wouldn't have met Nancy. And that brings me to the second part of my toast. Here's to Nancy, who introduced me to Bess, the greatest girl I've ever met." He held up his glass with one hand and reached for Bess's hand with the other.

Bess turned bright red, but Nancy noticed how her blue eyes sparkled as she looked up at Kyle.

"Here here!" Caroline said, and everyone murmured their assent as they clinked glasses.

Watching Bess and Kyle gaze into each other's eyes, Nancy wondered if there was any girl on earth as happy as her friend was at that moment.

Not a chance! Nancy decided.

Nancy's next case:

The heat is on in Key West. The sun is ablaze, the waters are boiling, and the temperatures are rising fast—with gold fever. Nancy sets sail on the *Lady Jane* in search of a wrecked Spanish galleon and a sunken treasure. The prize is twenty million dollars in gold, silver, and jewels, but the cost is even higher: one crew member has already paid with his life!

The police charge Sean Mahoney, owner of the *Lady Jane,* with murder, but Nancy suspects a setup. Beneath the surface of the expedition passions run deep and dangerous, and she's determined to bring out the truth. Greed, betrayal, and revenge are circling like sharks, and Nancy's diving straight into the deadly churning waters . . . in *Sea of Suspicion,* Case #85 in The Nancy Drew Files™.

The future is in the stars . . .
the possibilities unlimited . . .
the dangers beyond belief . . .
in
the pulse-pounding new adventure

THE ALIEN FACTOR

A Hardy Boys and Tom Swift™ Ultra Thriller

Tom Swift has caught a falling star—a visitor from outer space who is as beautiful as she is strange. But his secret encounter has set off alarms at the highest levels of government. To check Tom out, a top-secret intelligence agency sends two of its top operatives: Frank and Joe Hardy.

But when the alien is kidnapped, Frank and Joe and Tom realize they have to work together. They're dealing with a conspiracy that stretches from the farthest reaches of space into the deepest recesses of their own government. The fate of the country and the planet could rest on uncovering the shocking truth about the girl from another world!

COMING IN JUNE 1993